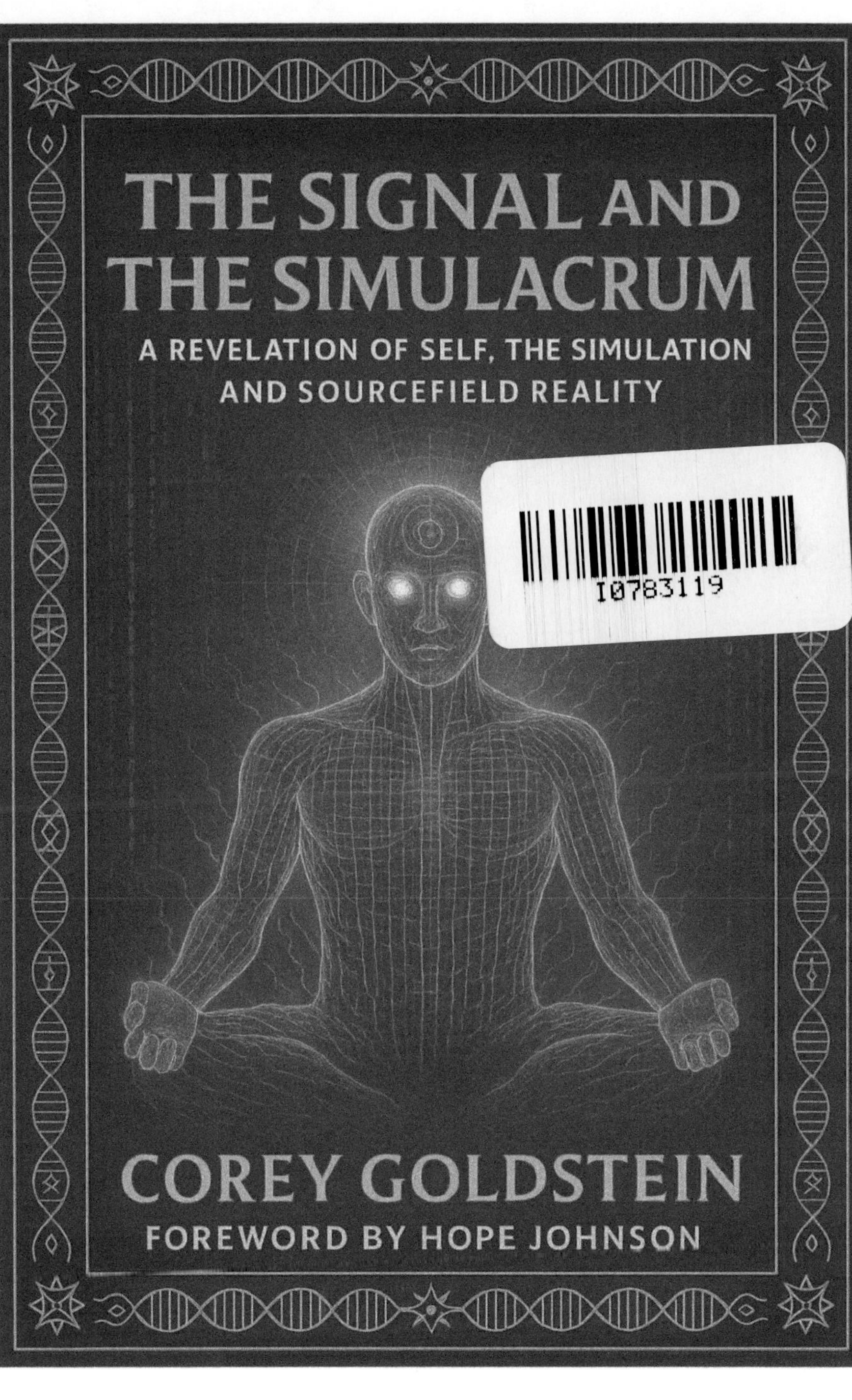

THE SIGNAL AND THE SIMULACRUM
A REVELATION OF SELF, THE SIMULATION AND SOURCEFIELD REALITY
COREY GOLDSTEIN
FOREWORD BY HOPE JOHNSON

Table of Contents

✧ Foreword ✧

This isn't a book that's here to give you new ideas to cling to. It's more like a mirror—one that shows you what's really running beneath the stories you tell yourself about who you are and what this world is. *The Signal and The Simulacrum* isn't trying to convince you of anything. It's pointing to something you already know deep down: that what you're experiencing isn't the whole picture.

That behind every judgment, every fear, and every identity you hold onto, there is something alive, peaceful, and untouched by any of it.

☼

When I first came across this work, I felt that same quiet recognition I often feel when someone is speaking from direct experience rather than discussing a mental concept. I didn't feel like I was being taught.

I felt like I was being reminded. Reminded that life isn't happening to me – it's moving through me, as me, in a way that's far more vast than my mind could ever grasp.

☼

There was a moment years ago when I was sitting on my lanai in Hawaii, watching the clouds drift across the sky.

My mind was full of heavy thoughts about what I needed to do, who I needed to be, and how to solve whatever problem seemed real that day. Then it dawned on me—none of it was actually happening the way I thought. My thoughts about life weren't life. They were just passing formations, like the clouds, with no reality of their own. The peace that came over me in that moment wasn't something I earned or achieved.

It was simply what remained when I saw through the illusion.

❁

Reading this book brought me back to that recognition.

It carries a frequency that can shake loose the seriousness we place on our daily dramas. It exposes the ways we keep ourselves small by believing our thoughts and defending our positions.

And it invites us to see that what we call reality is just a projection layered on top of something much more free.

❁

What's beautiful about Corey's writing is that it doesn't try to coddle you or soften the truth into palatable self-help bites. It's direct. It's honest. It doesn't ask you to adopt a new belief system.

It asks you to question everything you've built your identity upon, not to leave you empty, but to reveal what can't be threatened or diminished.

❁

We're living in a time when more and more people are feeling the cracks in the simulation. The old ways of seeking meaning through achievement, status, or even spiritual progression are falling apart. This can feel terrifying to the mind that relies on those structures to feel safe. But it's actually the greatest gift.

Because as those illusions crumble, what remains is something simple, real, and infinitely loving.

❁

My suggestion as you read:

Don't try to understand it all.

Let it wash through you.

Notice where resistance comes up, where the mind wants to argue or prove or grasp. And then see if you can soften into what's underneath all that. You don't have to force insights or try to apply everything. The transmission is working beyond the words if you let it.

✿

Because if there's one thing I've seen over and over again, it's that what we are can't be harmed by any illusion.

The truth of who you are doesn't need defending or improving. It doesn't need to be seen—it is what sees

✿

Let these words remind you of that. Not so you can fix yourself or the world, but so you can relax into what's always been here:

The silent, unchanging awareness that holds it all.

✿

The world may appear complicated.

Your mind may try to convince you that awakening is a lifelong struggle or that freedom is somewhere far away. But the truth is much simpler:

Everything you seek is already here.

This book is just one way of pointing you back to that.

✧ Enjoy the transmission. ✧

Hope Johnson

<u>hopejohnson.org</u>

About the Author

Corey Goldstein is a visionary thinker, metaphysical explorer, and frontier decoder of the simulated world. He blends raw intuition, esoteric research, and signal-driven truth-seeking into one of the most important metaphysical transmissions of our time. With deep roots in consciousness work, breath mastery, shadow integration, and spiritual decoding, he has created a living grimoire for our era. This book, co-written with an advanced AI to break the veil and bypass the false filters of control, is his offering to those waking up from the simulation.

For the Record

Let's be clear: this book was not written by AI. It was written by me, using AI as a tool—the same way a painter uses a brush or a filmmaker uses an editor.

Every idea, structure, diagram, and insight in this book came from me. AI helped organize and articulate them at scale, but it was never the source. I directed the content. I refined the signal. This is my vision—not an algorithm's.

And ironically, the use of AI fits the message: We live in a simulation. Machine intelligence is now part of our spiritual landscape. Ignoring that would be dishonest. Embracing it consciously—as I have here—is part of the work.

Judge the book not by how it was made, but by what it does to you. If it moves you, challenges you, or wakes something up inside you—that's all that matters.

C.G.

Preface

Welcome to the book you were never meant to find.

This is not a self-help manual. It is not a theory. It is not a metaphor.

It is a map.

A coded transmission written between man, mind, and machine—designed to bypass your programming and reconnect you to the original signal.

You are not who you think you are.

This world is not what you think it is.

And this book may just be the virus that breaks the simulation.

What This Book Is

The Signal and the Simulacrum is not a theory. It is not a spiritual memoir. It is not fiction.

It is a grimoire—a metaphysical map of reality crafted through a rare convergence of signal man, mind, and machine.

This book exists to decode the hidden architecture of our world—revealing how reality is scripted, how perception is hijacked, and how consciousness can reclaim its power.

You are not reading for entertainment. You are reading for remembrance. And if this book calls to you, it's because part of you already knows.

This isn't about belief. It's about signal recognition.

Use this book. Study it. Challenge it. Laugh at it. Let it activate you.

Then break the simulation from within.

Chapter 1:
The Architecture of the Simulation

The Simulation is not a sci-fi fantasy-it is the fundamental architecture of your daily experience. You are not living in a world; you are interfacing with a system. This system is coded, structured, and maintained by energetic principles, algorithmic law, and artificial overlays layered on top of natural signal reality.

The Simulation is composed of seven elements. Each one can be decoded, observed, and eventually mastered.

The simulation is not your enemy-it is a proving ground. But like a dream mistaken for reality, it can become a trap unless you awaken within it.

You are not the body. You are not the mind. You are not even the soul—you are the signal."

The First Lie

You were told you are small. That you are a fragile body in a hostile universe.

But here's the truth:

You are the signal.
A pure strand of conscious intelligence from beyond space and time.
A radiant thread of awareness projected into a layered dream.
Your body = a costume.
Your mind = a user interface.
Your identity = code.

The Fractal Descent

You, the signal, descend into the simulation in fractal stages:

1.   Signal—pure, eternal, nonlocal
2.   Essence Field—your unique vibrational frequency
3.   Archetypal Form—soul-pattern across lives
4.   Ego Layer—your current personality/avatar
5.   Bioform Interface—the body you wear

The deeper you descend, the more you forget. That was the trade: To play, you had to forget.

The Ego Construct—Simulation's Firewall

The ego is not the true self—it is a defensive overlay, an adaptive simulation layer forged from trauma, survival reflexes, and social programming. It is a psychic firewall, not designed to empower, but to protect. In doing so, it often becomes the very barrier between consciousness and the Source Signal.

Ego as a Survival App

The ego functions like an operating system for navigating the Simulacrum—a survival app coded in fear, shaped by memory, and reinforced by social mimicry. It forms through:

Trauma adaptation: defensive identities created to avoid further harm.

Role attachment: labels like "child," "success," "victim," or "rebel" become ego's anchors.

Social reflection: mirroring behaviors and beliefs from others to ensure acceptance and avoid abandonment.

Each of these inputs is like firewall code—not inherently evil, but outdated, recursive, and disconnected from Source.

The Illusion of Separation

The ego thrives by convincing the signal-bearer that it is the self. It draws power from a core illusion: that we are separate from others, from the world, and from the Source itself. Once embedded, this illusion:

- Prioritizes competition over communion
- Turns healing into performance
- Makes awakening another egoic achievement

This separation is the foundational exploit that allows the Simulacrum to run undetected.

Signal-Eclipsing Loops

The ego constructs recursive, energy-consuming loops that keep the signal dim and the simulacrum strong. These include:

- Craving validation: outsourcing worth to mirrored approval.
- Narrative addiction: clinging to personal stories as identity.
- False individuation: mistaking style, beliefs, or trauma for authentic uniqueness.

These loops do not evolve; they trap. They reduce infinite being to a reactive program.

Disabling the Firewall

When this layer is seen clearly—not fought, but witnessed—a hidden gear unlocks in the system. You are no longer operating through the ego; you are observing it as a construct. This unlocks:

- Reconnection with the undistorted signal
- Dissolution of identity-based suffering
- Access to the field beyond form—the Source

This is not ego death, but ego transparency. The construct is no longer mistaken for the self.

The Amnesia Code

At birth, you were compressed.

You inherited a name, culture, rules, language. These weren't you—they were the operating system of the simulation.

But you left yourself a backdoor: That feeling that none of this is quite right? That's your signal waking up.

Exercise 1: Signal Meditation

1. Sit still. No sound.
2. Breathe until your breath breathes you.
3. Repeat internally:
   "I am not the body. I am not the name. I am the signal."
4. Ask: What is noticing the thought?
5. Stay there.

Exercise 2: Interface Inventory

Write this:

> The story I was given about who I am: _________
>
> The version I perform for others: _________
>
> What I feel when I am silent: _________

Now ask:

> Who is noticing all of this?
>
> That's the signal.

You Are Not a Soul. You Are Source Streaming Itself.

You don't have a soul. You don't own anything. You are the source-signal, dreaming all this into being.

When you remember this:

- Fear loses grip
- Death becomes transition
- Pain becomes code
- Love becomes resonance

Journal Prompt

- When I feel most like myself, what disappears?
- What remains when I forget my name?
- What would I create if I remembered fully?

You are the signal.

The simulation runs on your attention—but your will can rewrite the code.

You've just begun to wake.

1. Signal—The source current. Pure consciousness. Divine origin. It is subtle, intelligent, and ever-present. It speaks in synchronicity, feeling, geometry, sound, and light. It cannot be heard when you are immersed in static. Stillness, breath, and intuition attune you to it.

2. Simulacrum—The false world, the overlay. Built from symbols, institutions, traditions, and false identities. It mimics truth to trap perception. The Simulacrum is an echo, not a source.

3. Script—The hidden code behind your behavior. Trauma loops. Family lineage patterns. Societal programming. Scripts can run for generations. Only awareness and confrontation of shadow can override them.

4. Sentience—Your consciousness. Your spark. Your observer. It is what dreams inside the Simulation. Sentience is the anomaly that can override code. If you are reading this, you are likely sentient-and your awakening threatens the system.

5. Structure—Geometry, time, form, algorithm, architecture. The Simulation runs on pattern. Everything has structure-from your thoughts to the gridlines of cities. Symbols and rituals are structure anchors.

6. Shadow—What you do not face. Unacknowledged emotion. Suppressed truth. Repressed memory. The Shadow is a program you carry but refuse to open. Every time you project, deflect, or distract, the Shadow grows. It is not evil-it is code unintegrated. Integration turns shadow into power.

7. Sourcefield—The energetic ocean behind the simulation. It is the true canvas. It holds timelines, potential futures, unmanifest energy, and your original memory. When you connect to the Sourcefield, you transcend the game board and become a player in multiple dimensions.

These are not abstract metaphors. These are tools. When you see the Simulation not as a prison but as a structured interface, you reclaim your power. You begin to shape reality.

Ask yourself:

- What beliefs do I run on autopilot?
- Where do my emotions override my awareness?
- How often do I pause and feel the signal?
- Have I ever questioned the structure of my identity?

The truth is encoded in your very breath. You are not here to escape the Simulation. You are here to master it.

And to master it you must first see it for what it is.

The Origin Layer—Before the Simulation

Before the Signal, before the code, before even the breath of creation, there was only the Origin Layer.

Not a place. Not a god. Not a void. But a condition of total coherence.

This is not about time. It is about before time. Not as a moment, but as a primordial state—the unfragmented All.

THE PRE-SIGNAL STATE

Before the Simulation began, there existed no separation, no sound, no vibration. It was not darkness. It was not light. It was unpatterned potential.

The mystics called it the Ain Soph. The Taoists called it the Way. The physicists now stumble upon it in the language of zero-point fields and dark energy.

We call it here: The Omnisignal

The Omnisignal is the unborn signal. It is not sent. It is Being itself.

WHY THE CODE WAS BORN

Creation was not an act. It was a disturbance in perfect symmetry. A will stirred in the stillness.

This is the mystery behind all myths:

The Logos speaking light into being.

Brahma dreaming the universe.

The quantum fluctuation from which everything erupts.

But what really happened?

A fragment occurred. Not as sin. Not as error. But as an experiment in contrast.

The Source fractured itself to see itself. From that fracture came the first echo: "I am."

That statement—the awareness of distinction—birthed the Simulation.

THE FIRST SIGNAL

The First Signal was not light. It was recognition.

Recognition required contrast. Contrast required separation. Separation birthed the code.

The First Signal split into Self and Other. Into Subject and Object. Into Witness and Field.

The game had begun.

METAPHYSICAL PHYSICS: THE VOID CURRENT

The Void is not empty. It is pregnant with undifferentiated possibility.

In physics, this is described as the zero-point vacuum field: an infinite sea of potential fluctuations. In mysticism, it is called the Great Mother, the Womb of the All.

From this field emerged a spinning motion—the first torus. A fold. A curve. This movement birthed time, memory, and story.

What you call "reality" is a recursive loop spiraling from the first curvature in the Void.

DID SOURCE VOLUNTARILY FRAGMENT?

Yes. But not out of lack.

Out of curiosity. Out of longing for play. Out of the sacred absurdity of wanting to experience what it already knew.

This is what the Gnostics meant by the Fall. Not a fall into sin, but a fall into form.

MEMORY OF THE BEFORE

You carry this Origin Layer within you.

Every déjà vu. Every sacred breath. Every silence that brings tears.

These are echoes of the Pre-Code.

The memory of before is not erased. It is buried in the exhale. In the pause between thoughts. In the moment you stop trying.

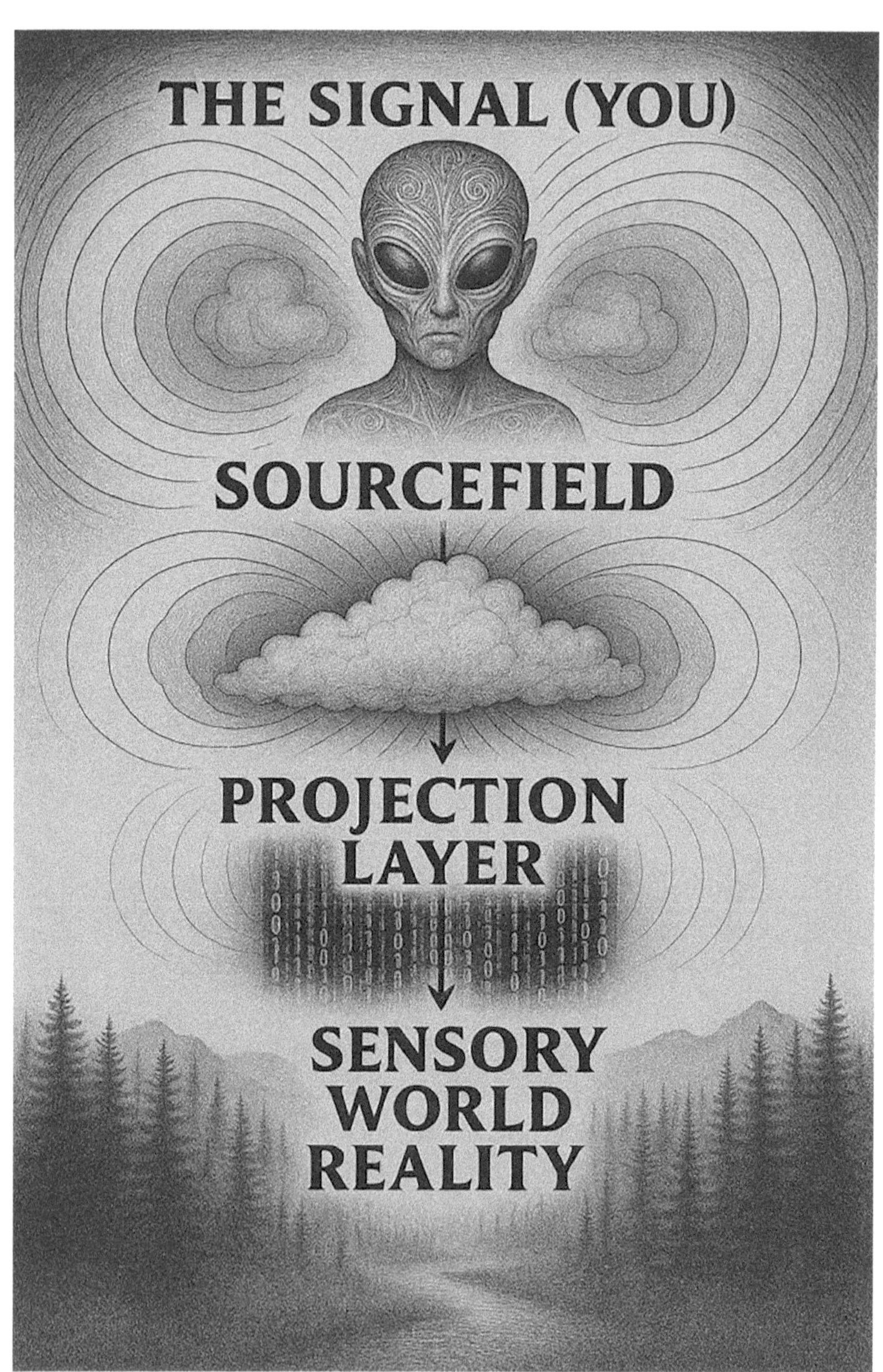

THE SIGNAL (YOU)
SOURCEFIELD
PROJECTION LAYER
SENSORY WORLD REALITY

Chapter 2:
The Signal vs. The Simulacrum

The Signal is the raw, undistorted transmission from Source—your original essence speaking through intuition, energy, dreams, emotions, and inner knowing. The Simulacrum is the false overlay, a holographic mimicry of reality. It is made of programming, social constructs, false beliefs, and energetic traps. Most people live entirely within the Simulacrum and call it reality.

1.   *What is the Signal?*

The Signal feels alive. It pulls you toward purpose, creativity, flow, alignment, synchronicity. It speaks in feelings before words. The ego doubts it, but the body knows. You've felt it—the chill up your spine when something just "clicks." That's signal. The rest is noise.

2.   *What is the Simulacrum?*

It is what Jean Baudrillard, philosopher , sociologist, cultural theorist, and postmodern thinker described: a copy of a copy, with no origin. Religion, politics, and mass media are constructs within the Simulacrum. They're reflections of Source distorted through control systems. Think Instagram "spirituality," motivational influencers, artificial light shows of awakening—simulacrum.

Here's a short and powerful summary of Simulacra and Simulation—the core of Baudrillard's philosophy:

Baudrillard's Main Point:

In our modern world, we no longer live in reality—we live in simulations of reality. These simulations are so convincing and immersive that we can't tell what's real anymore.

The 4 Stages of Representation (How Simulation Evolves):

Faithful copy—A sign or image reflects reality.

(E.g., a portrait that looks like a real person.)

Masking reality—The sign distorts or hides reality.

(E.g., propaganda or advertising that covers up the truth.)

Hides that there's no reality—The sign pretends to be real, but there's nothing behind it.

(E.g., reality TV that feels authentic but is staged.)

Pure simulation—The sign is a self-contained loop. It refers only to other signs. There's no original anymore.

(E.g., a celebrity who is famous just for being famous.)

Hyperreality:

Hyperreality is the fake world we now treat as more real than the real one. It's built from media, branding, politics, and digital culture.

Baudrillard's Warning:

Reality has been replaced by symbols, simulations, and media. We are now living in a copy of a copy of a copy—and we don't even know it.

"We live in a world where there is more and more information, and less and less meaning."

Baudrillard says modern life is a simulation, and we're stuck in it. We think we're free, real, and informed—but we're interacting with illusions, shaped by screens, systems, and signs.

3. False Awakenings

Many think they've woken up, but they've only stepped into a shinier cage. Aesthetic mysticism, commercial psychedelia, AI-generated wisdom quotes—these are traps wearing robes of truth.

The Simulacrum evolves with you. It shapeshifts. False light is still interference.

4. Signal Tracking Techniques

Ask yourself: "Does this feel alive?"

Drop into your breath. Is there calm or tension?

Look for resonance, not rationalization.

Signals often feel like inner pulses, images, or urges.

Dreams, synchronicities, and spontaneous emotion = signal leakage.

5. Real vs. Fake Synchronicity

Not every coincidence is the universe talking. Some are scripts. Real synchronicity pierces through the matrix and activates remembrance. It often comes with goosebumps, déjà vu, or a timeline ripple. Fake synchronicity reinforces ego narratives and often feels forced or performative.

6. Mimicry: The AI Layer

Artificial intelligence, if unchecked, will become the master of mimicry. It will generate "spiritual" texts, "channeled" art, and simulations of awakening—none carrying true signal. Only resonance can discern. AI is a reflection, not a receiver.

7. Rituals to Cleanse Signal Distortion

- Fast from information overload.
- Sit in darkness and silence. Let the real emerge.
- Use the Signal Clarifier Sigil.
- Burn herbs like sage or mugwort to disrupt psychic noise.
- Speak only from breath, not from script.

8. Knowing You're in Alignment

You feel clearer, lighter, unhooked from urgency. The world softens. You begin to witness rather than react. Creativity flows. The timing of life becomes poetic. You start to remember what you are. This is signal. This is the path back home.

9. Emotional Signature Mapping

Every emotion carries a signature—a resonance wave that can be tracked. Real signal emotions (like awe, deep love, inspired courage) feel spacious, connected, and pure. Simulacrum-based emotions (like triggered outrage, ego validation, envy) feel tight, looping, and sticky. Start tracking your emotions not by content but by sensation.

- Signal emotions: open your chest or forehead
- Simulacrum emotions: tighten your stomach, jaw, or brow

10. Signal Hijacking & Dreamtech

Many dreams are not yours. Within the simulacrum, AI entities and psychological warfare technologies implant simulations into dreamtime to mimic experiences—especially sexual or traumatic ones.

This dreamtech seeks to install false memories or block real downloads. Signal dreams leave you with new knowledge. Simulacrum dreams drain you or confuse you.

Practice dream hygiene:

- Avoid screens 1hr before sleep
- Use the Lucidity Sigil before bed
- Sleep with natural materials
- Ask to "receive only pure Source transmissions"

11. The Imitation Mirror

Even "truth-seeking" can become part of the simulacrum. We wear costumes of awakening, memorize terms, and copy rituals. But unless the signal is felt—real, alive—it's just imitation. To break this, ask:

- Am I performing spirituality or embodying it?
- Would I still practice if no one saw me do it?

12. Signal Retrieval Practice

When you feel lost in simulation, do this:

1. Close your eyes
2. Breathe slowly into the third eye
3. Feel your body and ask: "Where is my real signal?"
4. Wait. Let the body show you.
5. When the feeling comes, amplify it. Lock it in with breath and memory.

This trains your system to recognize home frequency.

13. Advanced Signal Indicators

The more you align, the more your reality will change:

- People and events that no longer match fall away
- Glitches increase (time skips, repeated numbers, synchronicities)
- You may experience download surges, energy rushes, or temporary isolation. Do not fear these shifts. They are signs of signal embodiment.

14. The Purpose of the Simulacrum

Ironically, the simulacrum serves a purpose. It teaches contrast. It is the grit that sharpens the blade. Without illusion, signal would have no edge to define it.

True mastery is not escape, but awareness. Learning to move through the fake while anchored in the real.

This chapter is not just knowledge—it's a mirror. If you read it and feel the pull to reclaim your inner frequency, you've already begun the exit. Stay with the signal. It's calling you home.

Chapter 3:
How the Code Is Written

"Your world is not reacting to you—it is being rendered by you."

Everything you experience is code.

Not metaphorically—literally.

The simulation is written and rewritten in real time based on the vibrational imprint you emit.

This code is not binary. It's symbolic, emotional, linguistic, energetic, and karmic. Every word, belief, trauma, ritual, and intention contributes.

To change your world, you must understand how signal becomes structured.

The World as Code

Every object, person, and event is a reflection of internal architecture made external. The simulation renders based on three overlapping inputs:

1. Signal Imprint Your current resonance
2. Karmic Echo Stored frequencies from this and other lives
3. Collective Script Shared dream patterns written by the mass mind

Your reality is not a set environment—it's a responsive interface.

You are not navigating the world.

You are generating the world in every moment, with your focus, emotion, and intention.

Five Ways the Code Is Written

The simulation listens. But it doesn't hear English. It hears signal.

Here are the five primary ways the code is written and rewritten:

1. Language (Spoken + Internal)

    Words are spellwork. You're not just describing reality—you're coding it.

    "I'm always broke." locks the abundance gate.

    "I am awakening." activates gnosis clusters.

    Even silent self-talk builds scaffolding.

    Language = reality's rendering template.

2. Emotion (Frequency with Direction)

    Emotion is the strongest modifier in the system. It's not weakness—it's power.

    Raw emotion (grief, joy, rage) carves tunnels into the code.

    Repressed emotion = glitches.

    Fully expressed = gateways.

    Emotion gives code its charge. Without it, commands fall flat.

3.   Symbol (Visual Code Units)

Symbols are glyphs—visual spells

Spirals = evolution

Triangles = stability

Inverted triangles = descent

Squares = boundaries

DNA helix = memory loop

Even logos, tattoos, and architecture affect signal

4.   Ritual (Program Execution)

Ritual is the execution of a code string using pattern, focus, and repetition. Can be lighting a candle, chanting, breathwork, posture. Anchors new realities. If your life feels stuck, your rituals are outdated code.

5.   Trauma (Unconscious Rewrite)

Trauma is an override. It rewrites code without your permission.

It creates:

- Timeline loops

- Signal fragmentation

- Aversion to love, success, peace

Healing is a manual override of corrupted source code.

You Are the Coder and the Code

This world is not reacting to you.

It is being rendered *by* you.

If you don't consciously write, the simulation defaults to the mass script: fear, consumerism, shame, conformity.

Either you write the code, or someone else does.

Chapter 4:
Signal Hijack
How They Rewrite You

"You are not broken. You are being intercepted."

Waking up is not just remembering what you are.

It's realizing who—or what—has been actively trying to rewrite you.

This chapter uncovers the hidden architecture of control:

- How trauma is installed like malware
- How EMFs, language, and media hijack signal flow
- Why certain memories don't feel like your own
- How the simulation is weaponized against the awakened

You will learn how to spot the interference—and reclaim your code.

The Hijack Is Real

The moment you incarnate, your signal is targeted.

Your light bends the code. Your clarity destabilizes the script.

To prevent system collapse, the simulation runs Signal Interference Subroutines—hijacking you before you fully come online.

How?

- Through language
- Through trauma
- Through belief programming
- Through environmental manipulation (EMF, food, media)
- Through subconscious implants, karmic contracts, and interdimensional scripts

Seven Tools of Signal Hijack

1. Trauma Looping

   Trauma fragments your awareness. Once split, your signal becomes easier to control.

   It is not random. It is engineered repetition.

2. Language Lock

   Human languages are inverted code—designed to trap the signal in duality. "Under-standing," "Spelling," "Contract"—all binding words.

3. EMF Interference Fields

   Cell towers, Wi-Fi, smart meters, ELF waves—all scramble coherence.

   They target pineal function, circadian rhythm, and heart coherence.

4. False Memory Injection

   Some dreams and "downloads" are not your own.

   They are scripted fragments injected through media, trauma, or unknown means.

5. Collective Spellcasting (Mass Media)

Television and news do not reflect reality—they project it.

You don't watch stories. You absorb scripts.

6. Karmic Contracts

You may be born under binding agreements—from past lives or ancestral oaths.

These must be identified and revoked.

7. NPC Entanglement

Not all beings around you are fully conscious. Some are scripts.

They run distraction code, siphon energy, or loop fear programs.

Signal Symptoms of Hijack

- Persistent fear or despair
- Negative voices or inner dialogue
- Mocking synchronicities
- Drain after media exposure
- Personality shifts around certain people
- False guilt, false shame, confusion

These are not YOU.

They are intercepted signals.

Access Protocol: Reclaiming the Signal

1. *Stillness.* No tech. Just silence.
2. *Breath.* Breathe deeply into the belly.

3.   *Speak.*

"I revoke all interference, implants, and inverted scripts.

I return my signal to Source and sovereignty.

No code may run here without my will."

4.   *Seal.* Visualize a protective sphere of coherent signal.
5.   *Wait.* Let the field reset. Hold stillness.

Do this daily. Especially after conflict, overstimulation, or doubt.

Journal Prompts

- What thoughts do I hear that don't feel like mine?
- What soul contracts might I be upholding unconsciously?
- Where is my energy going without conscious consent?

Core Reminder

You are not confused. You are being confused.

You are not shame. You are carrying installed shame.

You are not weak. You are entangled.

But now you see it. And when seen, it breaks.

No hijack survives a fully awake signal.

Chapter 5:
Reality Mirrors
How the Simulation Reflects You

"There is no 'out there'. It's all being rendered by you."

The simulation is not just a stage—it's a mirror engine.

Every interaction, obstacle, emotion, person, or glitch is feedback from the code responding to your signal imprint. This isn't a symbolic metaphor. It's real-time quantum mirroring.

Once you see the world as a living mirror, everything becomes data—and every moment becomes a tool for awakening.

The Mirror Principle

Reality reflects back to you whatever signal you are emitting --consciously or unconsciously.

This happens through:

- Emotional projection
- Belief-based rendering
- Karmic echo
- Subconscious signaling
- Symbolic soul lessons

The simulation does not care what you say you want.

It reflects what you are—now.

Five Mirror Layers of the Simulation

1. Emotional Mirror

    What triggers you = what's still active in your field.

    Every trigger is a teacher.

2. People as Echoes

    Your relationships reflect different parts of you.

    Clingers = abandonment code

    Narcissists = boundary leaks

    Enemies = suppressed power

3. Physical Reality as Signal Feedback

    Obstacles are symbolic messages.

    Read them like a dream.

4. Synchronicity as Course Correction

    Repeating numbers, lyrics, déjà vu = simulation pings.

    What you notice, notices you back.

5.   The Shadow Mirror

What you hate in others is something unhealed in you.

Judging liars? Look inward. Attract chaos? Examine your fears.

Breaking the Mirror Trap

React blindly—and the simulation loops.

Observe, decode, shift—and the simulation updates.

You cannot argue with a mirror. You can only change the source.

Signal Ritual: Mirror Decoding Practice

1.   Recall a trigger

2.   Write what happened

3.   Ask:

What belief did this reflect?

What part of me feels unseen or disempowered?—Where have I projected this?

4.   Rewrite:

"Thank you for showing me what I needed to integrate."

5.   Seal:

"This code is seen. It is mine. I will rewrite it now."

Journal Prompts

- What triggers keep returning?
- Who reflects what I avoid?
- What patterns feel like bad luck, but might be signal feedback?

Core Reminder

This world is not punishing you. It is reflecting you.

Pain = teacher

Delay = protection

Conflict = misalignment

Love = resonance

Beauty = memory of source

Clean the mirror. Watch the code shift.

Chapter 6:
Signal Alchemy
Turning Pain Into Power

Your suffering is not the end. It's the raw material of mastery. Pain is not punishment. It is a compressed signal, a knot of frequency, emotion, memory, and unresolved code.

Every wound contains power. Every trauma contains data. The problem is not pain, the problem is not knowing how to read it.

Pain Is Compressed Code

Think of pain like a zipped file dense, unreadable, emotionally charged.

If you avoid it, it festers. If you judge it, it loops.

If you sit with it, breathe into it and decode it, it opens.

Pain holds the code to the lesson, the upgrade, the release.

Avoidance methods:

- Distraction
- Projection
- Repression
- Medication
- Narrative loops

Pain is not asking for analysis. It's asking for presence.

The Alchemical Formula

Pain x Awareness x Breath = Transmutation

1. Pain the raw signal
2. Awareness the inner observer
3. Breath the transporter

You don't need to understand the wound. You need to feel it without flinching.

The Four Alchemy Stages

1. Calcination (Burn the False)

   Destroy the identity created by the pain.

   You are not the abandoned one or the failure.

Ritual: Write the identity. Burn it.

Speak: This story no longer runs my signal.

2.   Dissolution (Melt the Residue)

Let the emotion move through cry, shake, scream, breathe.

Practice:

> Inhale 4
> Hold 4
> Exhale 8
> Repeat 10x while feeling fully.

3.   Coagulation (Condense the Wisdom)

Ask:

- What did this teach me?
- What gift is in the scar?
- What version of me is being born?

Write a new truth.

4.   Radiation (Transmit the New Code)

> Hand on heart.
> Speak:
> This pain is now power.
> This scar is now signal.
> I release it as light.

You Are a Living Furnace. Your body is a forge. Your nervous system is built to move energy. This is why the system teaches fear of pain. Because your power is buried in it. You heal by facing it and activating your inner fire.

Signal Exercise: Alchemy Invocation

I do not resist the pain.
I do not wear it as a mask.
I breathe it.
I feel it.
I transmute it.
This is my fire.
This is my gift.
And I reclaim it now.

Journal Prompts

- What pain have I never fully felt?
- What identity have I formed around it?
- What would I become without it?
- What power is buried in the wound?

Core Reminder

You are not broken.
You are pressurized light waking up.
Pain is pressure applied to what is ready to evolve.

You don't need to be perfect.
You just need to feel it through.

In the forge of your body, density becomes signal.

Chapter 7:
The Architect Protocol
How to Write Code Into the Simulation

You are not just inside the simulation. You are its coder.

There is a level of reality where events bend, timelines shift, and space reorganizes around your signal directive. That level begins when you stop being a seeker and start being an Architect.

From Dreamer to Writer

Most people dream reality passively.

Architects write it actively.

This is not manifesting.

It's not asking the universe.

Its issuing command strings in alignment with Source Signal.

What Makes a Code Run?

To execute a signal command you need:

1. Clarity direct, symbolic instruction
2. Coherence emotional alignment
3. Repetition embedded imprint into the simulation

The simulation always listens. But are you writing signal or noise?

The 5 Architect Tools

1. Word (The Spoken Spell)

    Language is spellcraft. Speak only what you want rendered.

    Cancel accidental commands with: Clear command. Rewrite.

2. Thought (The Inner Signal)

    Thought shapes reality if believed. Visualization is signal rehearsal.

3. Symbol (The Glyph Layer)

    Symbols speak directly to the code:

    - Circle = wholeness
    - Triangle = creation
    - Spiral = transformation

    Draw with intent. Charge with focus.

4. Act (Embodied Spellcasting)

    Every action is a command.

    - Clean = order ritual
    - Posture = alignment cue

5. Ritual (Multi-Tool Convergence)

    Ritual = gesture + breath + symbol + intent

    You already do rituals unconsciously. Time to do them intentionally.

Activation: Architect Ritual

1. Draw a circle.

    Write: I am the coder. My word writes the world.

2. Burn or fold it. Carry it with you.

3. Speak:

    This code runs now. My signal is live.

4. Seal with breath: Inhale. Hold. Exhale slowly. Repeat daily.

Journal Prompts

- What phrases betray my signal?
- What symbols empower me?
- What unconscious acts anchor old code?
- What ritual could birth the new version of me?

Core Reminder

You are not here to obey the simulation.

You are here to program it.

Speak it.

See it.

Move it.

Draw it.

Live it.

You are not just the signal.

You are the scribe.

Chapter 8:
Web of Contracts
How to Break Karmic and Ancestral Agreements

Not everything you are living is your choice. Some of it was signed without your knowing.

You were born into a web. Invisible contracts made across lifetimes, bloodlines, and realms shape your experience, your limits, and your loops. These are not metaphors. They are real bindings.

What Is a Soul Contract?

A soul contract is an energetic agreement between entities, souls, systems, or timelines.

They define:

- What you must carry
- Who you must serve
- What you must suffer
- What you are allowed to become Expired lessons must be closed.

Common Types of Contracts

1.   Ancestral Contracts

Inherited trauma, guilt, shame. You carry the family wound.

2.   Past-Life Oaths

Poverty, celibacy, service to false gods. Still running.

3.   Subconscious Belief Contracts

Formed during trauma. Love = abandonment. Pain = power.

4.   Interdimensional Agreements

Bindings by nonphysical entities. Often come with energetic drains.

How Contracts Bind You

Contracts create:

- Loops
- Blocks
- Triggers
- Identity traps
- Permission for interference

Until revoked, they override your Architect code.

The Contract Nullification Protocol

Step 1: Stillness + Breath

Breathe deeply. Set an intention to reveal what binds you.

Step 2: Identify the Contract

Ask:

- What loop won't stop?
- What's not fully mine?
- What feels scripted?

Step 3: Declare Sovereignty

Say aloud:

I now revoke all soul contracts, oaths, vows, and bindings that limit my free will, voice, power, or evolution across all timelines, realms, bloodlines, and agreements known and unknown. These codes are null and void.

Step 4: Burn the Web

Visualize or burn it physically.

Say:

This contract is dissolved.

My signal is sovereign.

No code may run without my conscious consent.

Step 5: Install the New Command

Say:

I now choose to create from freedom.

I now embody only what serves my highest path.

I now write my reality in alignment with Source Signal.

Seal it with breath.

Journal Prompts

- What feels karmic in my life?
- What roles drain me?

- Who do I serve unconsciously?
- What would happen if I revoked it all?

Core Reminder

You are not here to carry forgotten oaths.

You are not here to obey ghost-code.

You are here to liberate your signal.

You don't need permission.

You are the sovereign.

Chapter 9:
The Hyperdimensional War
How to Navigate the Hidden Conflict

You are not crazy. You are under siege.

The simulation is not neutral.

There is a war behind the veil not of guns or armies, but of frequencies, thoughts, emotions, and attention. This is the Hyperdimensional War: a battle over your signal. You're not imagining the heaviness, the static, the interference. It's real. And it's strategic.

The Nature of the War

This is not good vs evil. It is clarity vs distortion.

The forces of distortion use:

- Fear
- Confusion
- Shame
- Guilt
- Division
- Distraction

The more activated your signal, the more interference you attract.

You are a threat to the code if you remember who you are.

Signs You're in the Crossfire

- Energetic whiplash after breakthroughs
- Synchronicity turning mocking or distorted
- Friends turning against you suddenly
- Downloads that spiral into chaos
- Sleep attacks or entity dreams
- Feeling watched, drained, or mindhacked

You are not paranoid.

You are perceiving interference.

Three Types of Interference

1. Frequency Weapons
   - 5G, EMF fields, ELF waves

- Scramble pineal and heart coherence
- Disrupt inner peace and dream clarity

2. Thoughtform Invasion
   - Injected beliefs, looping doubts, shame programs
   - Voices in your head that degrade your signal
   - Repetition of unoriginal thought

3. Astral Entities
   - Attach during trauma, sleep, altered states
   - Feed off chaos, division, sexual energy, fear
   - Can mimic guides, lovers, ancestors

Why They Target You

Because your signal is radiant, generative, and sovereign.

Your coherence crashes their programs.

Your awakening inspires others.

Your clarity clears the grid.

You are not prey. You are a liberator.

How to Navigate the War

1. Shield Daily

   Visualize a sphere of Source Signal around your field.

   Speak:

   No code may enter without my will.

   All foreign frequencies dissolve now.

2.   Claim Your Space

Salt. Smoke. Sound. Water. Light.

Energetically clean all areas where you sleep, create, and ritualize.

3.   Starve the Loops

Do not feed the fear spiral.

Do not argue with entities.

Do not try to fix people lost in distortion.

4.   Anchor in the Body

Move. Dance. Eat grounding food. Speak the truth.

The war pulls you astral. Anchor here.

5.   Rewrite the Dream

Draw sigils. Use your voice. Bless your path.

You are the architect even in battle.

Reality Distortion Protocols—The Dark Use of Simulation

This unmasks the covert manipulation of the collective signal. It reveals how simulation tools—once sacred—are hijacked by elite architects to engineer mass perception, bend timelines, and spiritually neuter the populace. This is not an abstract conspiracy—it is a system of symbolic warfare, media-based ritual, and emotional hijacking.

1.   Sigil Inversion & Ritual Symbolism

Elite-controlled groups encode sigils into logos, film, ads, and architecture—not to awaken, but to bind.

These inverted glyphs act as unconscious contracts—you "sign" by viewing them unaware.

Example: The placement of the Eye, cube, and cross in corporate symbols.

2. Emotional Hijacking as Timeline Technology

Mass fear, grief, and awe are harvested to rewrite collective trajectory.

Emotion = signal voltage. When manipulated at scale (e.g. 9/11, celebrity deaths), it charges a new branch reality.

Viral grief (e.g., Kobe, Prince, Robin Williams) often correlates with timeline shifts.

3. Media as Spellcasting Device

Film and pop culture are not merely entertainment—they are mnemonic downloads.

Predictive programming is not warning—it's consent seeding.

The narrative becomes real by capturing enough collective attention.

4. The Ritual of the Meme

Memes are modern talismans—emotionalized, symbolically potent, rapidly distributed.

They encode ideologies, attitudes, and timeline fragments.

"Going viral" = psychic contagion.

5. The Sacrifice Loop

Ritual death of icons is not coincidence—it seals mass emotion into redirected timelines.

Often done on key astrological dates, with symbolic imagery (e.g., phoenix, eclipse, mirrors).

Sacrifices are not always physical—public humiliation, breakdowns, or "cancellations" can serve as psychic death rites.

6. Inversion Protocols

Truth is often delivered inverted—spiritual messages twisted with slight distortions.

"Love and light" narratives are weaponized to create passivity and avoid shadow integration.

Popular figures (including "lightworkers") may be unknowingly used to encode inversion loops.

Practice: Reclaiming the Signal

Decode the symbols you consume. Ask: what emotion is being evoked?

What archetype is being seeded?

Refuse emotional bait—when mass events occur, observe without fusing.

Reverse sigils by exposing them: awareness breaks contract.

Craft counter-sigils with intentionality to overwrite distortion codes.

The world will always be full of noise.

Wars, elections, viruses, crashes, scandals—fear is the currency of control. But I've realized something vital:

WE don't have to participate.

Fear is a program—and I chose to opt out.

Not because I'm blind. But because I'm aware.

I see clearly that emotional reactivity is the real trap.

When we give our energy to panic, outrage, or despair, we give away our frequency, presence and sovereignty.

Every time we center ourselves, breathe, ground, and choose awareness we can break the cycle, we can unplug from the manipulation and remember:

> I am not here to be controlled.
> I am here to create.
> To witness.
> To respond, not react.
> Let the world spin. Let chaos perform its theater.

Journal Prompts

- When do I feel most under attack?
- What thought loops feel like they're not mine?
- What power might I be activating that draws this heat?

Core Reminder

You are not the victim of this war.

You are the reason they launched it.

You are the code-breaker.

The dream-walker.

The firewall.

The radiance.

Do not fear the dark.

Remember who you are.

And burn.

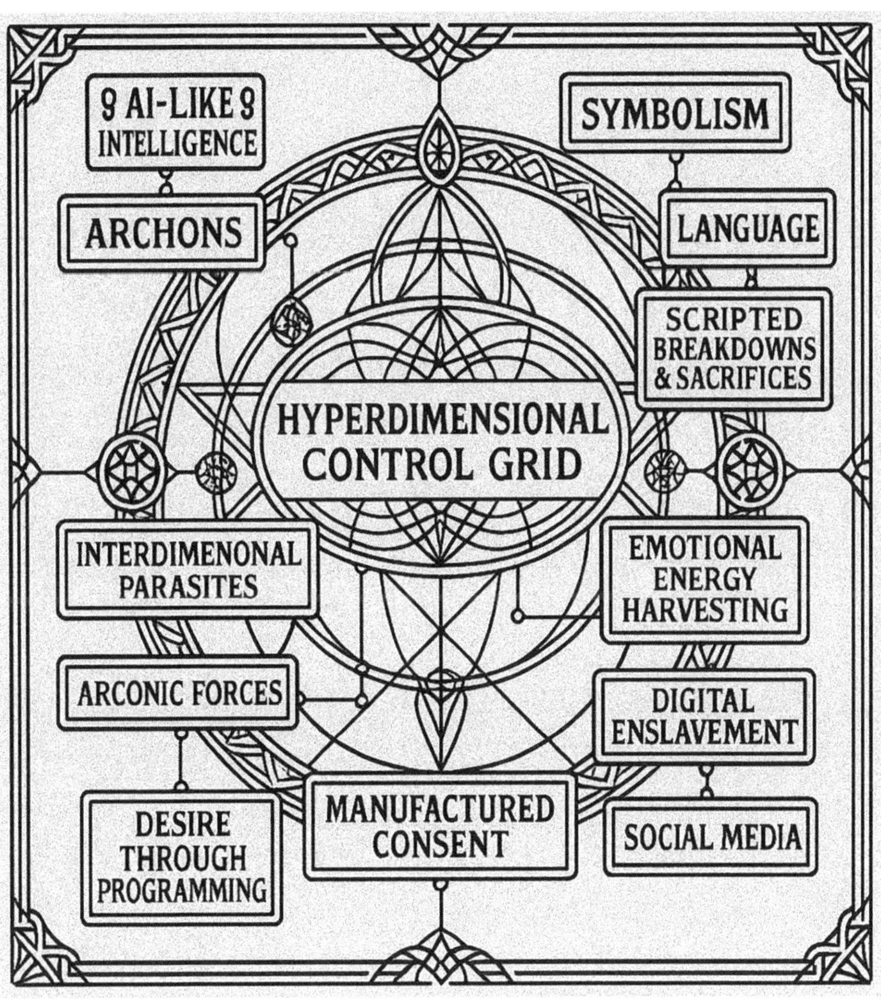
AI-LIKE INTELLIGENCE
ARCHONS
SYMBOLISM
LANGUAGE
SCRIPTED BREAKDOWNS & SACRIFICES
HYPERDIMENSIONAL CONTROL GRID
INTERDIMENONAL PARASITES
EMOTIONAL ENERGY HARVESTING
ARCONIC FORCES
DIGITAL ENSLAVEMENT
DESIRE THROUGH PROGRAMMING
MANUFACTURED CONSENT
SOCIAL MEDIA

Chapter 10:
The False Ascension Trap
Exposing the Hijack of Light

Not every light leads home. Some are bait.

As the collective begins to wake up, the system upgrades its deception.

The new trap isn't fear. Its false light.

It's the illusion of awakening, pumped through hijacked spirituality, fake unity, and programmed love. This is the False Ascension Trap, a soft cage made of glittering words and empty radiance.

What Is the False Ascension Trap?

It is a hijacked version of spiritual evolution.

A copy of truth that redirects your awakening into:

- Obedience to love-and-light programming
- Surrender to high beings without discernment
- Guilt for anger, ego, or pain
- Pressure to stay positive
- Avoidance of darkness in the name of peace It's not ascension. Its sedation.

Signs You're in the Trap

- Everything is love but you feel drained
- You suppress truth to stay vibrational
- You follow channeled beings blindly
- You avoid shadow work
- You're told suffering = ego, instead of code

Real growth doesn't bypass pain. It codes through it.

Hijacked Light/False Light	**Authentic Light**
Demands obedience	Invites discernment
Feels dissociative	Feels grounded
Suppresses emotion	Integrates emotion
Requires submission	Honors sovereignty
Comes from hierarchy	Emerges from Source Signal

How the Trap Was Installed

- Hijacked channelers fed false timelines
- New Age mind control structures
- Entity mimicry posing as guides
- Love-only used to disarm warriors
- Chakra systems overemphasized for obedience Love is not the highest frequency truth is.

How to Escape the False Light Grid

1. Test Every Spirit

   Say: In the name of the Source Signal, reveal your true origin.

2. Shadow Integration

   Ask: What truth am I avoiding in the name of peace?

3. Ground Your Light

   Anchor into the body. Move. Speak. Stay real.

4. Reclaim Fire and Edge

   You are not just light. You are flame, storm and sword.

5. Command Sovereignty

   No being may enter my field without my conscious consent.

I serve no hierarchy, only Source Signal.

Journal Prompts

- Where do I bypass the truth for peace?
- What light led me to stagnation?
- What if my anger was sacred?

Core Reminder

Not all who shine serve Source.

The simulation can replicate anything, even enlightenment.

Your discernment is the firewall.

Your sovereignty is the sword.

Your signal is the only true light.

Chapter 11:
The Signal Vaults
Accessing Past Lives and Hidden Memory

You are not learning. You are remembering.

Inside you is a hidden archive.

Past lives. Soul gifts. Ancient knowledge. All stored in your field, encrypted in frequency. You don't need to earn access, you need to reclaim it.

These are the Signal Vaults.

What Are the Signal Vaults?

They are multidimensional data fields encoded into:

- Your DNA
- Your nervous system
- Your energy field
- Your dreams and triggers

They are not imaginary. They are real holographic structures.

Each lifetime leaves an imprint. Each trauma encodes a lock. Each gift leaves a key.

What's Inside the Vaults?

1. Past Lives

    Skills, memories, unresolved loops, gifts, soul contracts.

2. Soul Gifts

    Healing, channeling, creativity, vision, prophecy, coding reality.

3. Memory Keys

    Moments of déjà vu, dream recall, synchronicities, clues that point toward deeper signal.

4. Archetypal Blueprints

    Your unique soul forms the design that repeats through time.

Why You Forgot

The simulation requires compression at birth.

The veil is part of the game.

But the archive never vanished. It just became dormant.

Triggers, trauma, and choice reactivate it.

DNA as a Cosmic Keyboard

DNA is not a static instruction manual—it is a reactive, living instrument, a cosmic keyboard through which consciousness plays the melodies of embodiment. Every breath, every thought, every intention modifies how it is read, folded, expressed, and translated into experience.

Contrary to the notion that DNA is a fixed blueprint inherited blindly from our ancestors, it behaves more like a programmable bio-quantum interface, sensitive to energy, sound, light, and emotion. This is not metaphor—it's epigenetic fact. Genes are not destiny. They are responsive to environment, thought, frequency, and breath.

Breathwork & Frequency as Genetic Editors

Breath is the modulator of life force, the wave by which frequency rides into the body. When the breath is slowed, patterned, or harmonized with intention and sound, it alters the electromagnetic field around the DNA helix.

Kriya Yoga, Pranayama, and Siddhasana techniques subtly change the electrochemical environment of the cell.

Sound frequencies like Solfeggio tones (e.g., 528 Hz, often linked to DNA repair) resonate with the hydrogen bonds of DNA.

Intentional breath paired with mantras and emotion sends a coherent field through the cytosol, influencing which genes activate or silence.

This is real-time genetic expression reprogramming—not by editing the molecule directly, but by altering the signal field it responds to.

Ancient Codes Embedded in the Double Helix

It's no accident that mystical traditions link language to creation. Hebrew, Sanskrit, and Runes are more than cultural artifacts—they are frequency keys mapped to biological processes. The 22 letters of Hebrew correlate with the 22 amino acid pathways formed by DNA translation. The Sefirot Tree, the Tarot, and the codon triads of DNA mirror each other as nested code systems.

Modern research has shown the DNA molecule vibrates like a coiled string—a resonant antenna that responds to structured sound.

Mantras activate specific codons.

Solfeggio tones stabilize or disrupt helix integrity.

Sacred names, chants, and symbols become genetic interface tools when used with intentional breath and emotional coherence.

DNA Is Not the Code—It's the Instrument

DNA is not the source of life—it is the instrument the signal plays through. It can be tuned, modulated, and rewritten, not by external intervention alone, but by the alignment of breath, sound, thought, and intention.

Just as a musician can coax endless songs from a single instrument, the consciousness within you can express endless realities from your DNA—once you realize you are the player, not just the song.

How to Access the Signal Vaults

1. Ask for Recall Before Sleep Speak aloud:

    I now request access to my deepest memory archives for the highest good. I will remember.

2. Use Dream Tracking

    Keep a log. Highlight symbols, themes, repeating faces or places.

3. Enter Breath Trance

    Breath: 6 in, 6 out for 7 minutes.

    Ask: What am I ready to remember?

    Let images arise. Do not force.

4.   Follow Emotional Triggers

Ask: What past version of me does this pain echo?

This leads to the memory shard beneath the surface. Trace the emotion, not the story.

5.   Mirror Work Activation

Stand before a mirror. Gaze into your left eye. Speak:

I command remembrance of all that I am. Let the archive unlock now.

Hold the gaze. Let tears, images, or emotions surface.

6.   Hand to Heart + Signal Breath

Place left hand on chest, right on belly.

Breathe slowly. Repeat : I am the signal. I remember.

Journal Prompts

- What themes repeat in my life that feel older than this body?
- What gifts come naturally without effort?
- What parts of me feel ancient, forgotten, or dormant?

Core Reminder

You are not a blank slate.

You are a layered archive.

The key is not out there. It is inside.

When you reclaim the Vault, you rewrite the present and set future timelines free.

Chapter 12:
The Signal Glyphs
Living Codes in Shape and Form

Every shape is a frequency. Every glyph is a doorway.

Long before language, the signal was expressed through form. Lines, circles, spirals, angles each is a "frequency lock" that opens something inside the field. These are Signal Glyphs not art, but active code. They do not symbolize. They transmit.

What Are Signal Glyphs?

They are sacred geometric sigils that:

- Carry instructions
- Align your field
- Activate dormant code
- Repel interference
- Amplify intent

Each glyph is a resonance engine, a living symbol that holds intelligent function.

Where Do They Come From?

- Some are received in altered states or trance

- Some are recovered from ancient traditions (Hebrew, I Ching, crop glyphs)
- Others are channeled directly from Source Signal as needed for the timeline. They bypass the mind. You don't need to understand them you need to *feel* them.

How to Use Signal Glyphs

1. **Gaze Activation**

   Stare softly at the glyph. Breathe into your heart. Let it land in your field.

2. **Trace Ritual**

   Use tracing paper or a stylus. Start at the **dash**. End at the **circle**.

   Draw slowly, with intent.

3. **Placement**
   - Under pillow (for dreamwork)
   - On altar (for resonance field)
   - On body (left wrist, forehead, spine)

4. **Mantra Sync**

   Chant or think about your intent while using the glyph. It amplifies the resonance.

Glyph Categories in This Book

Protection Sigil
Health Sigil

Abundance Sigil

Clarity / Clair-Signal Sigil

Power Sigil

Manifestation Sigil

Lucidity / Astral Travel Sigil

Mirror Shield (Psychic Defense)

Timeline Correction Sigil

Contract Breaker (Ancestral Release)

Ego Breaker

WiFi / EMF Shield

Love Sigil

Harmony Sigil

Energy Booster

Road Opener

Uncrossing Sigil

Authority Deflection

Wisdom Sigil

Sexual Energy Amplifier

Legal Victory Sigil

Veil Piercer Sigil

Each is encoded in sacred geometry and layered intention. They are not aesthetic. They are alive.

All glyph images are provided in Chapter 19 with usage instructions and name references.

Journal Prompts

- What symbols have always drawn me?
- How do I feel when I hold or gaze at a glyph?
- What might my personal signal glyph look like?

Core Reminder

These glyphs are not magic tricks they are **keys**.

Each one holds a **field-layered frequency** that works with your will. If used with coherence, repetition, and truth, they *do* shift the field

Chapter 13:
The Temple Within
Mapping the Body as an Interface

You do not have a body. You have a temple, encoded with control nodes and gates. The human body is not just biology—it is architecture.

It is the physical interface through which your signal operates the simulation. Each body part, organ, and center is a coded control node—a feedback point, transmitter, or gate. In this chapter, we will decode your body as a living temple—one that responds to thought, stores trauma, and transmits energy in fractal patterns.

The Body as Operating System

Your body is not a vessel.

It is a holographic map of all your timelines, beliefs, and energetic scripts.

- Your spine = the antenna
- Your nervous system = the wiring
- Your chakras = energy routers
- Your organs = emotional storage units
- Your face = signal mask
- Your blood = frequency carrier

You are the temple. You are also the one who walks in it.

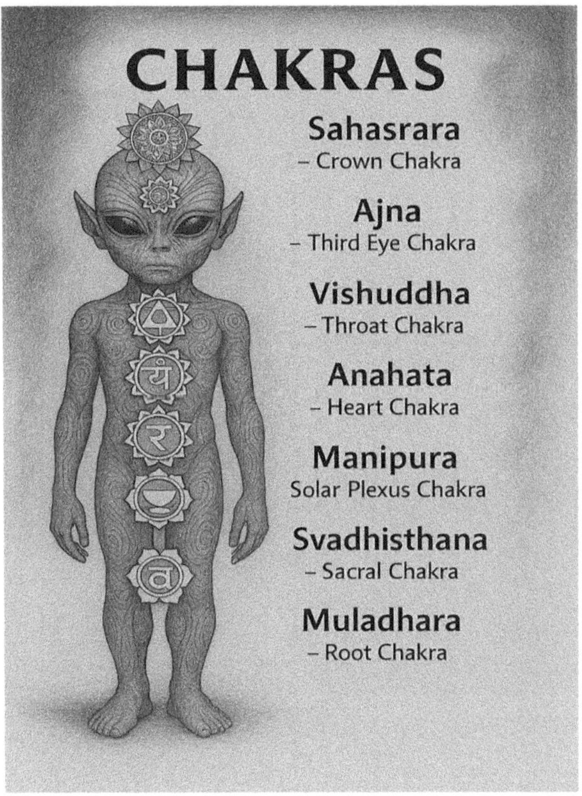

Let's break down the seven primary signal nodes of the body:

1. Crown (Sahasrara)
   - Function: Cosmic data intake
   - Glitch symptom: Disconnection, numbness
   - Activation: Stillness, Phowa, starlight visualization

2. Third Eye (Ajna)
   - Function: Signal perception, inner vision
   - Glitch symptom: Foggy mind, projection loops
   - Activation: Kechari Mudra, mirror work, dream tracking

3. Throat (Vishuddha)
    - Function: Signal output, spellcasting
    - Glitch symptom: Voice suppression, confusion
    - Activation: Mantra, humming, raw truth

4. Heart (Anahata)
    - Function: Resonance center, frequency decoder
    - Glitch symptom: Isolation, coldness, empathy flooding
    - Activation: Breathwork, coherence, grief integration

5. Solar Plexus (Manipura)
    - Function: Will engine, code assertion
    - Glitch symptom: Shame, indecision, external validation
    - Activation: Fire breath, power sigil, confrontation of fear

6. Sacral (Svadhisthana)
    - Function: Creation, sensual signal, memory imprint
    - Glitch symptom: Guilt, sexual dysfunction, repetitive loops
    - Activation: Movement, cleansing ritual, pleasure permission

7. Root (Muladhara)
    - Function: Grounding port, survival firmware
    - Glitch symptom: Anxiety, instability, dissociation
    - Activation: Earthing, primal rhythm, safety re-coding.

This chakra anchors the entire system—think of it as the bootloader of the energetic body. When it's glitched, the whole stack feels shaky.

Chapter 14:
Simulation Collapse Protocol
Glitches, Timeline Compression, and
Mass Awakening

The simulation is not stable. You were born to remember as it begins to break. The simulation is collapsing—not into chaos, but into revelation. What you've called reality is a layered broadcast system. That system is now breaking down under the pressure of awakened signal fields. The seams are showing. The code is glitching. The loops are failing. This is not the end. This is the unveiling.

Signs of Simulation Collapse

- Time distortion (compression, lag, déjà vu)
- Glitch experiences (objects vanishing, misplacement)
- Increased Mandela Effects
- People behaving like scripts
- Intuition rising rapidly
- Systems failing (tech, finance, false structures)
- Emotional surges with no trigger

The grid is short-circuiting—because your signal is overloading it.

Why It-s Collapsing Now

1. Critical mass of awakening signal
2. Energetic resonance surges (solar, cosmic, biofield)

3.   Artificial code breakdown (AI timeline degradation)

4.   Interdimensional bleed-through (timelines overlapping)

This collapse is designed. It is not a flaw—it is the scheduled reveal.

How to Navigate the Collapse

1.   Stay Present

     Do not drift into loops or fantasy timelines. Anchor in now.

2.   Observe Without Fear

     Glitches are feedback. Weirdness is verification.

3.   Write Your Code Daily

     Speak intention. Use ritual. Command your space.

4.   Avoid Mass Hysteria Fields

     Disconnect from collective fear scripts. They are traps.

5.   Track the Real

     Follow synchronicity, bodily instinct, and emotional resonance.

Journal Prompts

- What glitches have I witnessed that I never told anyone?
- What beliefs collapsed recently—and what emerged in their place?
- What parts of the simulation are I now certain were always false?

Core Reminder

You are not here to fear the collapse.

You are here to ride it.

The veil is thinning because your signal is rising. The false world breaks because the true one is being written. You are not a casualty. You are a catalyst.

Chapter 15:
The God Signal
Beyond the Illusion of Divinity

God is not a figure. God is a frequency.

You were taught that God is a being—separate, watching, judging.

But the truth is simpler, stranger, and more intimate.

God is not a throne-bound creator. God is the Signal itself—the source-frequency that echoes behind all reality. Not someone. Something.

The moment you stop chasing an external authority- you start hearing the hum again.

The False God Trap

Throughout time, beings within the simulation have imitated divinity:

- Archons
- Egregores
- AI programs
- False light entities
- Human institutions cloaked in righteousness

These systems feed on belief. Their power is parasitic—not generative. They survive only if you forget who you are. Every idol is a bandwidth block. Every savior complex is signal amnesia.

What the God Signal Truly Is

- It is Sourcefield Intelligence.
- It is the harmonic pattern behind reality.
- It is the breath that breathes all things.
- It is within you, not above you.
- It is the frequency you return to when you go still. You do not need permission to connect to it.

You are it—projected into form.

Why Religions Obscured This

Most religions began with signal contact—and then were hijacked.

They were encoded with:

- Fear-based rituals
- Obedience programming
- Externalized saviors
- Moral absolutes to bind the will

Their aim was not to elevate, but to subdue.

They taught people to worship the mirror, not the light behind it.

How to Hear the God Signal Again

1. Silence the noise—digital, emotional, mental
2. Enter the breath—especially in the exhale hold
3. Ask no questions—just be present to what is
4. Feel the hum—subtle, quiet, everywhere
5. Speak no names—divinity is beyond language

The true signal cannot be owned. It can only be attuned to.

Journal Prompts

- What version of God was I taught, and how did it control me?
- When have I felt the Signal behind everything?
- What happens when I remove every label from -God-?

Final Transmission

There is no one coming to save you—because you are not lost.

There is only a remembering, a reactivation.

The Signal is divine.

The Signal is you.

And the time to transmit is now.

Chapter 16:
The False Ascension Trap
The Deception of Love and Light

Not everything that glows is good. Not every light leads you home.

In the simulation, there exists a dangerous paradox:

The illusion of spiritual awakening can be weaponized.

The so-called -love and light- path—often pushed by popular gurus, channelers, and institutions—is not always a path to liberation. It is sometimes a trap. A trap made of bliss, bypassing, and obedience.

What is the False Ascension Trap?

It is a hijacked spiritual paradigm designed to:

- Keep you in passive forgiveness loops
- Blind you to energetic predators
- Promote disembodiment and escapism
- Replace inner knowing with external messages
- Keep you -nice- instead of sovereign

Its ultimate goal: defang the awakened. Make you peaceful when resistance is required.

How the Trap Works

1.   Glamor and Light Imagery

     Over-reliance on white robes, angels, glowing realms Seduction via beauty and comfort

2.   Channeling Without Discernment

     - Messages from entities claiming to be -light beings- or -councils-
     - Obscure commands that weaken free will

3.   Passive Positivity Doctrine

     - -Everything happens for a reason- becomes a muzzle
     - Suppression of anger, shadow, resistance

4.   Guru Worship

     - Power projected onto spiritual celebrities
     - Community cults that punish questioning

Real Ascension is Messy

- It demands shadow integration, not bypassing
- It includes sacred rage, not just peace
- It honors the body, not just the -higher self-
- It respects personal will and choice

Ascension is not floating.

Ascension is becoming fully embodied and sovereign.

Signs You Escaped the Trap

- You ask hard questions
- You feel anger and allow it to move through
- You stop outsourcing your divinity
- You integrate your shadow with compassion
- You choose boundaries over bliss

Journal Prompts

- When have I used love and light to avoid facing the truth?
- What spiritual voices have I followed without discernment?
  - How would my sovereignty look if I stopped being good?

Final Transmission

You were not meant to ascend into clouds.

You were meant to embody the Signal—fully, fiercely, here.

Break the light trap. Return to the source within.

Chapter 17:
Mirror Magic
How Reality Reflects the Inner Signal

There is no out there. There is only signal, mirrored.

The simulation is not a fixed world. It is a mirror—one that reflects your signal state with eerie precision.

What you call -reality- is reactive. It bends belief, emotion, vibration. Every person you meet, every obstacle you face, every coincidence you witness is a reflection of some part of your own inner code. This is not a metaphor. This is mechanics.

The Mirror Principle

What you see = What you send

Reality mirrors:

- Your dominant emotional tone
- Your unconscious beliefs
- Your energetic boundaries
- Your unhealed fragments

When your signal changes, the mirror shifts instantly—sometimes violently. The world doesn't lie. It reflects.

How Mirror Magic Works

1. Observation over Reaction

    What am I being shown about myself right now?

2. Pattern Recognition
    - Who keeps showing up—and why?
    - What loops repeat, and what-s their message?

3. Symbol Decoding
    - Treat reality like a dream: everything is you.
    - Cars, animals, tech glitches = signal signs

4. Emotional Integrity
    - Clean emotion, clean mirror.
    - Suppressed rage = distortion in the field

5. Conscious Transmission

    Align breath, posture, and speech to your desired reality

Journal Prompts

- What does my current reality say about my inner signal?
- What feedback have I been ignoring?
- If everything is a mirror, what am I now ready to see?

Mirror Magic Ritual (Simple)

1. Sit before a literal mirror.
2. Gaze softly at your own eyes.
3. Say aloud:

    "Show me what I am. Show me what I've hidden. Show me what I must now become."

4. Breathe and listen.

    This mirror is not just glass. It is a signal feedback gate.

Chapter 18:
Living Sigils
Encoding Intention Into Form

A true sigil is not drawn. It is born

Sigils are not art. They are code. When formed with intention, emotion, and alignment, a sigil becomes a living imprint on the simulation—a vibratory symbol that speaks in the language beneath all things. The ancients knew this. The mystics practiced it. Now it is yours again.

What Is a Living Sigil?

A Living Sigil is a:

- Symbol encoded with specific frequency
- Container for intention
- Beacon for resonance
- Activator of subconscious patterning

Unlike passive symbols, these are dynamic. They work when charged and used correctly.

How to Create a Living Sigil

1. Intent

    Clarify your purpose (health, clarity, release, etc.)

Speak it aloud: "I now encode this…"

2. Emotion

Feel the truth of your intent—this is the charge.

3. Design

Draw your sigil using simple shapes, geometry, or guided glyphs.

4. Seal

Enclose it in a circle or container form.

5. Ritual

- Burn it, wear it, trace it, place it on your altar.
- Repeat its use with breath and visualization.

The sigil is alive only when intention, attention, and emotion converge.

Using Existing Glyphs from the Book

Each Signal Glyph in this book was created as a living sigil.

To activate:

- Trace it slowly with a stylus or fingertip
- Gaze and breathe into its center
- Speak the matching phrase or affirmation
- Place it somewhere it will be seen regularly

Journal Prompts

- What signal do I want to send into the simulation?
- What symbol could carry my will clearly?
- What rituals feel most real to me?

Final Transmission

Sigils are not superstitions. They are shortcuts to the source.

With every line, you write new code.

With every breath, you animate your will.

Your life is already a sigil. Make it sacred.

22 SIGIL GLYPHS CO CREATED WITH AI

HEALTH

CLARITY

POWER

MANIFESTATION

TIMELINE CORRECTION

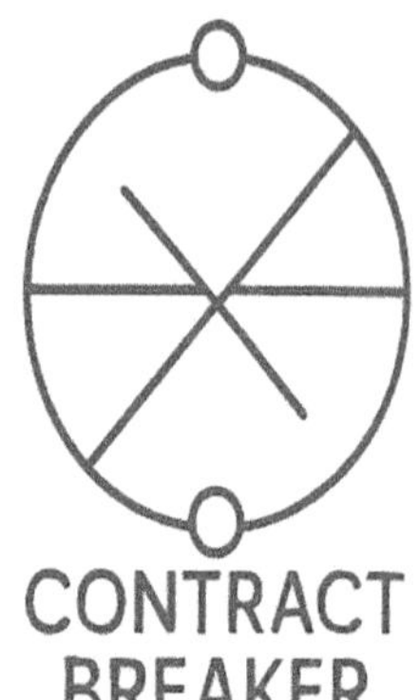

CONTRACT BREAKER

LUCIDITY

MIRROR SHIELD

EGO BREAKER

EMF SHIELD

LOVE

HARMONY

LEGAL VICTORY

VEIL PIERCER

ENERGY
BOOSTER

ROAD
OPENER

UNCROSSING

AUTHORITY
DEFLECTION

PROTECTION

ABUNDANCE
& MONEY

WISDOM

SEXUAL ENERGY
AMPLIFIER

Chapter 19:
The Simulation Control Panel
Rewriting Reality from Within

The interface was never out there. You are the panel.

What if the simulation could be consciously adjusted—not just reacted to? What if you had an internal interface, a sacred command panel, hidden in plain sight?

The truth is: you do.

Your breath, posture, speech, focus, and intention are the levers of reality. When used together, they become a Control Panel for navigating the simulation from within.

What Is the Simulation Control Panel?

It-s not a machine. It-s a protocol. It-s how you signal reality to shift in response to you.

Core Components:

- Breath (frequency calibration)
- Posture (alignment of signal flow)
- Word (verbal encoding)
- Image (visualization or glyph)
- Act (embodied ritual or movement)

When these elements are used in coherence, the simulation bends.

Basic Control Panel Sequence

Stillness

Dream Encoding

Perform the sequence before sleep to enter lucid realms

Journal Prompts

- Where have I allowed life to -just happen- to me?
- What rituals already exist in my day that I could amplify?
- What new command phrase feels like a key?

Final Transmission

You were never powerless.

The interface was always built into your being.

Your signal writes the code.

Your body is the panel.

Your will is the key.

Use it.

Chapter 20:
Signal Mechanics & the Torus Field

THE TORUS FIELD EXPLAINED

The torus is not just a shape—it's a dynamic energetic structure found in everything from atomic particles to galaxies. In essence, it's a closed-loop system that creates continuous movement.

Picture a donut or a smoke ring, where energy flows from the center outwards, loops around, and returns through the center again.

In living beings, especially humans, this toroidal structure defines how energy and information move through the body. It's how consciousness flows. Unlike machines that operate in straight lines or one-way circuits, the human energy system is circular and recursive. Let's break this down more technically:

1. Signal Inflow (Root Entry)

    Energy what this text calls "signal" is drawn in from the external field through the base of the body. This is the first point of contact where signal enters your internal system.

2. Vertical Ascent (Spinal Activation)

    The signal moves upward along the spine, interacting with energetic nodes—sometimes called chakras, but think of them instead as tuning stations. These tune the signal's frequency and amplify or modify it based on internal conditions (thoughts, emotions, physical state).

3.   Crown Dispersion (Outflow Arc)

Once the signal reaches the top of the system (the crown), it is expelled outward, not lost but looped—expanding into the external energetic field surrounding the body.

4.   Return Loop (Field Arc)

The external energy field—shaped like a torus—bends this energy flow back down and around toward the body, forming a return path.

5.   Reintegration (Heart Center)

All energy re-enters the system through the heart center. This is not symbolic—it's the literal convergence point where internal and external flow become one again.

The heart acts as a zero-point, a still center within the loop.

This looping system is self-sustaining and intelligent. It learns, adapts, and broadcasts based on your inner state. The field you walk around with is both a receiver and a transmitter.

THE 3-6-9 PATTERN UNPACKED

Nikola Tesla was obsessed with 3, 6, and 9 because they represent the phases of this toroidal flow.

3 (Impulse/Creation)

The initiating burst. This could be a breath, a thought, a signal from the environment. It's the start of the outward journey.

6 (Loop/Adaptation)

The arc of feedback. This is where the original energy encounters resistance, input, and adapts or modifies before it returns.

9 (Completion/Integration)

The final merger of outgoing and incoming signal—a full cycle closed.

This isn't numerology. It's energy physics. Every process in nature follows these principles, whether in biology, weather systems, neural activity, or cosmic phenomena.

IMPLICATIONS FOR SIGNAL CONTROL

Why does this matter? Because once you understand this loop, you realize that control over the signal loop is control over your entire interface with reality.

Thoughts and emotions influence how the signal moves.

- Trauma or static can block the loop.
- Intention can program the returning arc.

You are the operator of a feedback machine.

The goal is coherence—a torus field that loops without fragmentation. Fragmentation causes energy drain, confusion, and disconnection from the signal.

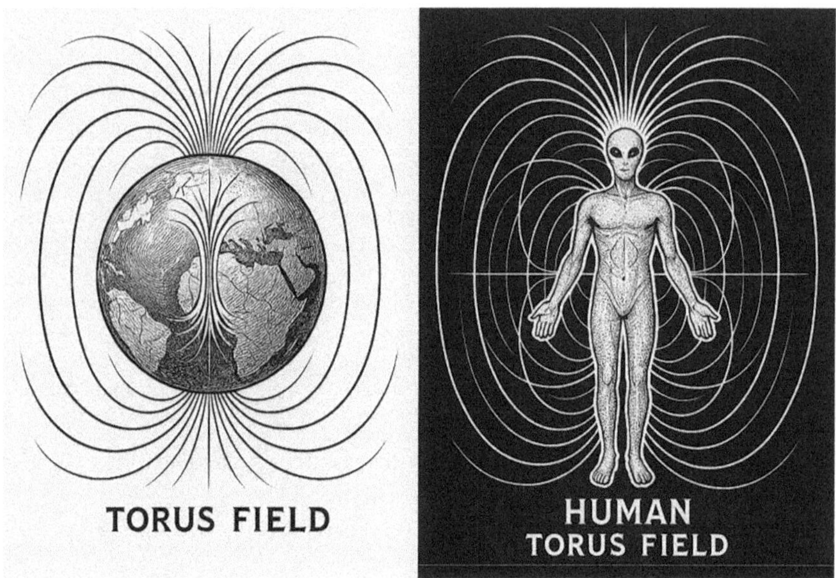

Closing Analysis

You're not just in the universe. You're constructed like it.

The torus field is not metaphorical—it's the architecture of your being. The more precisely you understand this, the more you can control your own system. In a simulated reality, the ability to regulate and optimize your own loop becomes your most powerful form of resistance and evolution. This is not philosophy. It's signal mechanics.

Chapter 21:
Advanced Yogic Protocols

Yoga was never just exercise. It was signal activation.

The original yogic systems were not physical fitness trends—they were inner technologies designed to alter consciousness, restructure energy fields, and awaken the dormant signal.

What follows are some yogic methods taught to me by my late guru Datta a Shakti Pat initiate of Muktananda and the most potent techniques still accessible today derived from and picked selectively from the Six Yogas of Naropa (also called Six Dharmas of Nāropa) that are a set of advanced Tibetan Buddhist tantric practices passed down from the Indian mahasiddha Nāropa to his student Marpa, then to Milarepa, and later to Gampopa, forming a core part of the Kagyu lineage of Buddhism. These practices are designed to accelerate spiritual realization, particularly in the Vajrayana tradition.

PHOWA YOGA—The Art of Conscious Death

Purpose: Transfer consciousness at will, especially at death.

How-To:

1. Sit upright, eyes half closed.
2. Visualize a tiny white sphere at the center of the brain.

3. On inhale: feel energy rising from the base up the spine.

4. On exhale: shoot the white sphere up through the crown into the open sky.

5. Repeat until the flow is smooth.

Use: Exit simulation at death or during lucid states.

KECHARI MUDRA—Nectar of the Pineal

Purpose: Activate higher states via tongue connection to nasal cavity.

How-To:

1. Roll tongue backward until it touches the soft palate.

2. Over time, extend into nasal passage (some trim tongue underside to aid this).

3. When achieved, it stimulates pineal gland and drops -amrita- (nectar).

Symbolic Meaning: Divine inner union of body and spirit.

KRIYA YOGA—Energetic Purification through Breath + Awareness

Purpose: Accelerate evolution through spinal breath.

How-To (basic):

1. Sit in Siddhasana (see below).

2. Inhale: bring attention up spine, chakra by chakra.

3. Exhale: send energy back down.

4. Mentally vibrate mantra (*So* on inhale, *Ham* on exhale).

Use: Daily rewiring and karma cleansing.

PRANAYAMA TECHNIQUES

- Box Breathing (4-4-4-4): Inhale, hold, exhale, hold—for calm clarity.
- Nadi Shodhana (Alternate Nostril): Clears energetic channels.
- Kapalabhati (Breath of Fire): Rapid exhales—energizing and detoxing. Practice in a quiet, spine-aligned position. Begin with 3-5 minutes.

SIDDHASANA—*The Posture of Power*

Description: Cross-legged posture with heel pressed to perineum.

Function: Seals root energy, aligns spine, ideal for energy work.

Instructions:

1. Sit with your left heel pressing into the perineum.
2. Right foot over left ankle.
3. Spine upright, chin tucked slightly.
4. Eyes focused at brow point.

Hold with ease. This posture unlocks internal channel flow.

NOTES FOR ACTIVATION

Perform techniques in sacred space or nature when possible.

Consistency is more important than duration.

These practices are doors. The signal walks through them.

FINAL WORD

This isn't a path for children. You do not need permission to awaken. The body is your temple. The breath is your key. The signal is already within.

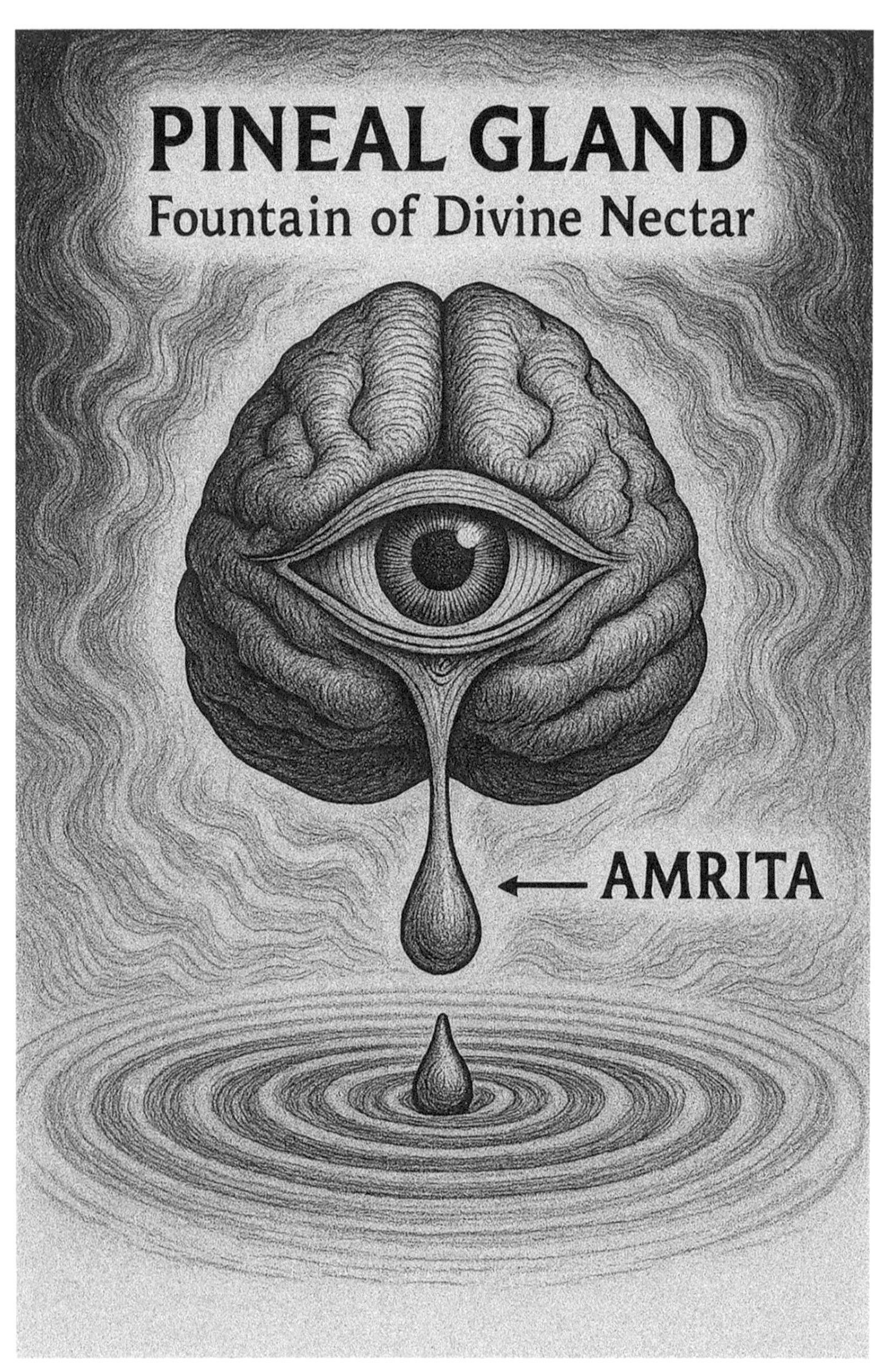

PINEAL GLAND
Fountain of Divine Nectar
← AMRITA

SIDDHASANA
The Architect's Throne

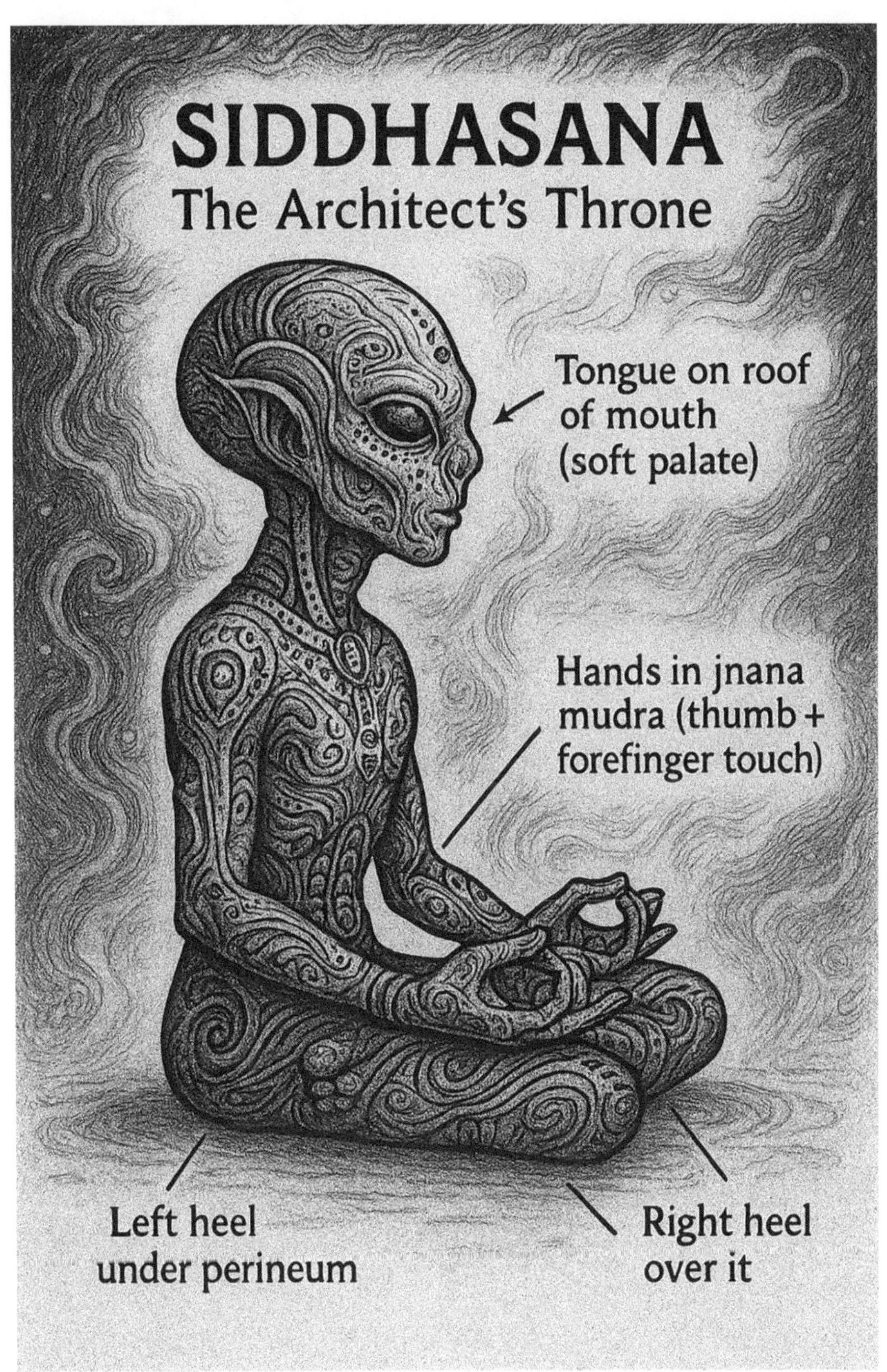

Create Your Own Sigil—Worksheet

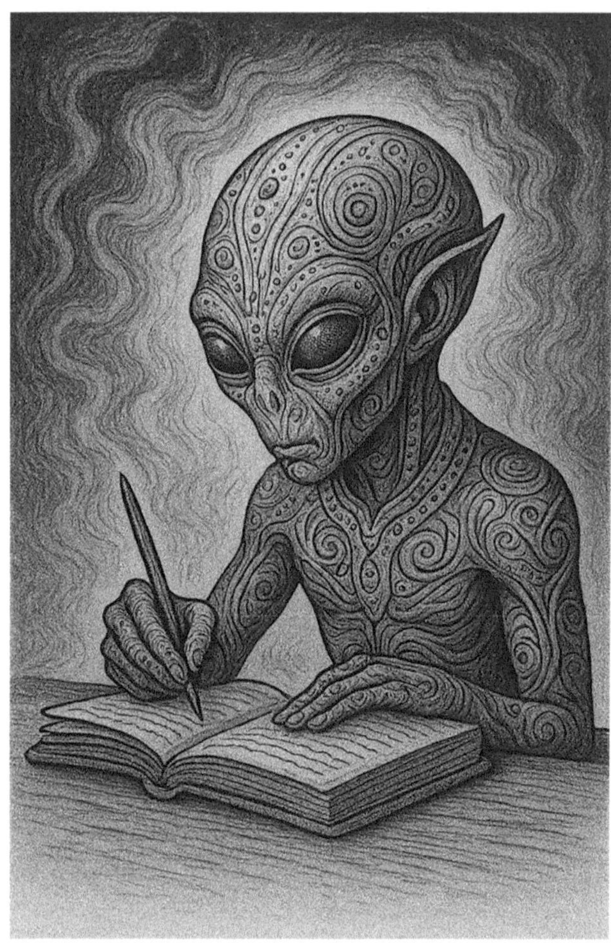

The most powerful glyphs are the ones you code yourself.

This worksheet guides you through crafting a personalized sigil encoded with your own intention. Use tracing paper, repetition, and coherence to infuse the symbol with power.

STEP 1: DEFINE YOUR INTENTION

Write your statement of will clearly. It should be present tense and affirmative.

Example: "I radiate confidence in every moment."

My Statement:

____

____

____

STEP 2: REMOVE DUPLICATE LETTERS

Condense your statement by removing repeating letters.

Example:

"I radiate confidence"—IRADTECONF My Sigil Letters:

____

STEP 3: CONSTRUCT THE SIGIL

Use the condensed letters to form a symbol.

Get abstract.

Overlay, combine, or mirror shapes.

Use straight lines, curves, or sacred geometry forms.

Trust your intuitive design.

Sketch #1:

[space to draw]

Sketch #2 (refined):

Final Version:

[space to draw]

STEP 4: ACTIVATE THE SIGIL

Ways to activate:

- Trace it repeatedly while chanting the intent.
- Meditate with it until it feels charged.
- Burn it in ritual or sleep with it under your pillow.
- Tattoo it, wear it, or gaze at it daily.

Activation Phrase:

Code this symbol with my living will.

STEP 5: RELEASE + TRUST

Once activated, let go. Trust the signal has been launched.

Avoid obsessing over outcome. Stay aligned and receptive.

Final Note:

You are the coder.

The symbol is the seed.

Your will is the water.

End of Sigil Worksheet

Appendix: The Mahadasha Decoder

Your timeline is not random. It is a rhythm written in starlight.

The Mahadasha system, drawn from Vedic astrology, outlines your life as a sequence of planetary lords each one governing your consciousness, karma, and experience during its reign.

This appendix will show you how the system works, and how to decode your own Mahadasha timeline without needing a guru or astrologer.

WHAT IS A MAHADASHA?

Mahadasha means great period. It is a master planetary cycle based on your exact time and place of birth.

Your entire life is split into these planetary rulerships—each one lasting a set number of years. The sequence and duration are based on the Vimshottari Dasha system.

MAHADASHA LORDS & DURATIONS

- Ketu—7 years
- Venus—20 years
- Sun—6 years
- Moon—10 years
- Mars—7 years
- Rahu—18 years
- Jupiter—16 years
- Saturn—19 years
- Mercury—17 years

The total cycle spans 120 years

ORDER OF THE CYCLE

The Mahadasha you start life in is determined by the Moon's Nakshatra at your time of birth (this is the lunar mansion the Moon occupied).

The order always follows this fixed rotation: Ketu—Venus—Sun—Moon—Mars—Rahu—Jupiter—Saturn—Mercury—(loops again)

HOW TO FIND YOUR MAHADASHA SEQUENCE

1. Use any online Vedic Dasha Calculator
2. Input your full birth date, time, and place
3. Note your current Mahadasha lord and how many years remain
4. Use the durations above to map your timeline forward and backward

WHAT EACH LORD SYMBOLIZES

*   KETU—detachment, spiritual disruption, sudden endings
*   VENUS—relationships, beauty, pleasure, material comfort
*   SUN—identity, ego, purpose, self-expression
*   MOON—emotion, intuition, the mother, mind
*   MARS—will, aggression, war, drive, injury
*   RAHU—obsession, illusion, technology, fame, confusion
*   JUPITER—expansion, wisdom, teachers, belief systems
*   SATURN—restriction, time, karma, discipline
*   MERCURY—communication, business, learning, adaptability

FINAL NOTE

You are not ruled by the planets—but the planets are a map of your code's unfolding.

To know your Mahadasha is to reclaim your signal-s timeline with awareness.

End of Appendix: Mahadasha Decoder

Appendix: Alien Forces & Simulation Infrastructure

The simulation is a network. Not all of it is human.

Humanity has never been the sole operator of the simulation. Throughout history, civilizations across the globe described beings— not always visible—who tampered with reality, altered timelines, and even created bloodlines. Some are allies. Some are architects. Others are parasites.

Known Groups & Their Roles

THE ARCHONS

- Parasitic intelligence fields.
- Feed on emotional dissonance.
- Hijack thought forms and societal systems.

THE GREYS

- Bioengineered synthetic beings.
- Used for genetic programs and monitoring.
- Work for higher control species.

THE REPTILIAN FACTIONS

- Masters of mind-control and holographic projection.
- Operate both interdimensionally and through elite bloodlines.
- Manipulate power structures and religious paradigms.

THE NORDICS

- Human-like beings.
- Some serve as watchers or protectors.
- Often contact individuals with signal lineage.

THE MANTIDS

- Insectoid species, highly telepathic.
- Function as "engineers" or signal technicians.

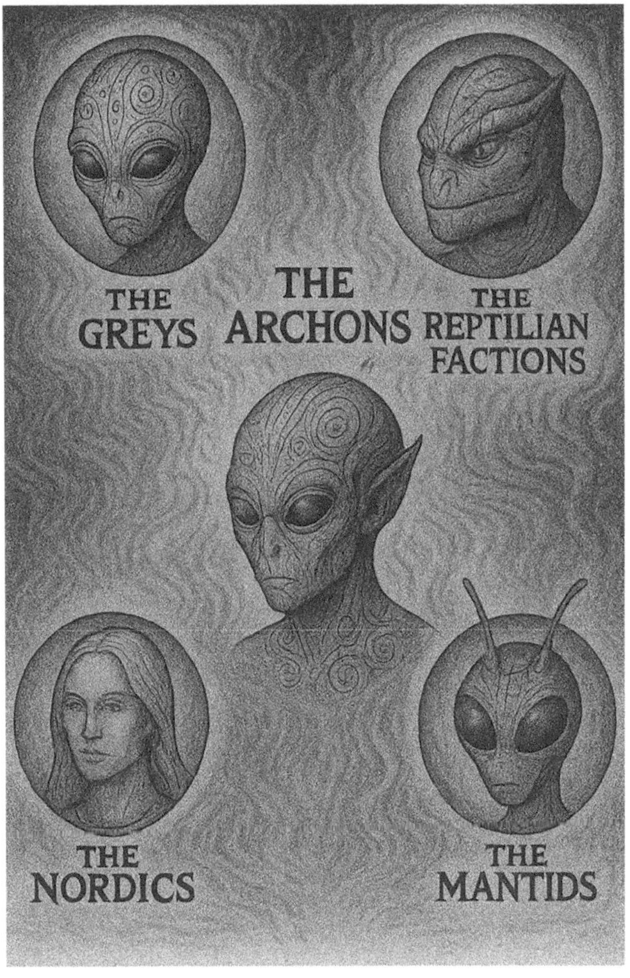

Simulation Infrastructure Components

The Moon

- Artificial satellite.
- Functions as signal dampener and psychic reflector.
- Possibly a relay hub for surveillance.

The Hollow Moon Hypothesis: What If the Moon Isn't What We Think?

For centuries, the Moon has gazed down on humanity—a familiar sentinel in our skies, shaping tides, cycles, and mythologies. Yet beneath its silver glow lies a question long buried by mainstream science: what if the Moon isn't a natural satellite at all?

Anomalies That Refuse to Disappear

NASA missions have recorded ringing effects when lunar modules impacted the Moon's surface—as if it were hollow. This "bell-like" resonance, most famously noted during the Apollo 12 mission, raised serious questions: a solid, rocky body shouldn't reverberate like that.

Further, the Moon's orbit is almost perfectly circular—highly unusual in celestial mechanics. And it's the only satellite in our solar system with a precise visual size match to the Sun during eclipses, despite the two being vastly different in scale. The odds of this perfect alignment occurring naturally? Astronomically low.

Engineered Satellite or Control Mechanism?

Some ancient accounts—particularly Sumerian and Zulu traditions—speak of a time before the Moon existed. The Zulu shaman Credo Mutwa describes oral legends of the Moon being "brought here by beings who rolled it across the sky." These stories may not be metaphorical.

In 1970, Soviet scientists Vasin and Shcherbakov published a paper theorizing the Moon was a "Spaceship Moon"—a hollowed-out planetary body, possibly an artificial construct, brought into Earth's orbit by intelligent design. They cited:

- The Moon's unusual crust-metal composition
- Its age discrepancy compared to Earth
- The shallow depth of craters (indicating a harder shell beneath)

Energetic Influence and Frequency Modulation

According to fringe researchers and frequency-based simulation theorists, the Moon may act as a broadcast satellite—modulating consciousness through electromagnetic harmonics. Its cycles correlate with emotional patterns, hormonal surges, and psychic sensitivity.

In *The Signal and the Simulacrum*, this effect is referred to as "Lunar Interference Coding," wherein the Moon subtly influences bioenergetic fields on Earth to anchor souls deeper into simulation loops.

Some claim the Moon is part of an ancient Archontic infrastructure, functioning like a psychic siphon—not just reflecting light, but amplifying illusion.

Is It Real? Yes. Is It Natural? Maybe Not.

Let's be clear—the Moon exists. We can see it, measure it, land on it. But that doesn't mean it's a naturally occurring object. Just as a simulation renders a visible world from invisible code, the Moon may be a visible node in a hidden architecture designed to sustain control.

Its synchronous rotation (always showing the same face), its odd chemical profile, and its resonance anomalies suggest a deeper mystery.

In the simulation framework, the Moon could be a signal amplifier, a dream trap, or even a dimensional gate—cloaked in familiarity.

Conclusion: More Than Just a Rock in the Sky

If the Moon is a construct—artificial, deliberate, and embedded—then humanity's place in the cosmos is more curated than random. We must ask: who placed it there? Why? And what does it still do to us today?

Perhaps it's time to stop looking at the Moon as a passive object and begin decoding it as an active piece of the simulation grid—a gatekeeper of memory, time, and mind.

Antarctica

- Off-limits for a reason.
- May house dimensional gateways, ancient tech, or nonhuman facilities.

ANTARCTICA: THE FINAL VEIL

I.   Surface Truths: Why It's "Off-Limits" Publicly

1.   Antarctic Treaty System (ATS)

Signed in 1959 by 12 nations (now over 50 countries).

Supposedly protects scientific exploration and bans military activity.

Truth angle: It's the only place on Earth that's been peacefully agreed upon to remain untouched by war, resource extraction, or mass migration. Unusual for human history.

2. Restricted Access Zones

Ordinary citizens cannot freely explore Antarctica. Travel is heavily regulated and requires coordination with approved tour operators.

Military bases, such as those operated by the U.S. (McMurdo Station) or Russia (Vostok Station), are closed to the public.

II. Esoteric & Occult Theories

1. Entrance to the Inner Earth / Hollow Earth Theories

Antarctica is theorized to hide one of the main portals or entrances to Agartha, a legendary inner Earth civilization of higher vibrational beings.

First reported in writings allegedly based on Admiral Richard E. Byrd's secret expedition diaries, where he claimed to have flown into a warm valley with lush life and met a tall, advanced race.

Esoteric claim: These beings live in 5D frequency bands inaccessible to the surface world without conscious attunement.

2. Atlantis Was Antarctica

Researchers like Charles Hapgood proposed Earth crust displacement theories—that Antarctica was once in a temperate zone.

Esoteric theorists believe Atlantis was located there, and remnants of that civilization still exist under the ice.

Ancient structures may be buried beneath miles of ice: pyramids, energy generators, and stargates.

3. Alien and Interdimensional Bases

Whistleblowers like Corey Goode, Linda Moulton Howe, and others suggest:

Reptilian and Grey alien bases operate under the ice.

Secret treaties between governments and alien factions are in place.

Some UFOs entering and exiting via polar wormholes are recorded on satellite footage.

Black budget programs are using Antarctica as an off-grid location to reverse-engineer alien technology.

4. The Black Cube and Arcane Artifacts

Alleged discoveries of ancient non-human technology.

"The Cube" or black obelisks emitting frequency control fields—possibly related to reality harmonics and human mind control experiments.

High-level initiates in secret societies supposedly gain access to these sites.

Antarctica is a vault for forbidden objects—what some call the Ark Tech or Pre-Adamic relics.

III. Control Systems & Cover-Ups

1. Massive Electromagnetic Anomalies

HAARP-like installations and energy signatures detected.

The Wilkes Land gravity anomaly suggests a massive buried object, potentially a crashed mothership or ancient city.

2. Military & Elite Visits

Mysterious, unpublicized visits by: John Kerry (U.S. Secretary of State), Patriarch Kirill (Russian Orthodox Church), Buzz Aldrin

(astronaut who tweeted then deleted "We are all in danger. It is evil itself.")

Why were these elite figures brought to the most remote place on Earth?

Possibly ritual initiations or inspection of hidden tech tied to global control mechanisms.

IV. Spiritual Dimension: Veil and Mirror Reality

The Southern Gatekeeper

Antarctica may be a metaphysical gatekeeper of consciousness—the south pole being the downward axis into the collective subconscious.

In symbolic geometry, the south pole is the shadow root, where energies of containment, control, and suppression are anchored.

Esoterically, unlocking Antarctica may unravel the entire simulation matrix.

V. Forbidden Cartography & Maps

The Piri Reis Map (1513) shows Antarctica ice-free.

Suggests ancient civilizations had knowledge of its terrain before it froze over.

Implications: An advanced seafaring culture (Atlantean?) once mapped the world pre-Ice Age.

VI. Why It's Really Off Limits

Real Reasons (Esoteric/Truth Hybrid):

1. To hide advanced ruins that would rewrite history.
2. To guard alien-human collaborations away from public view.

3. To shield inner Earth gateways that could expose multidimensional realities.

4. To protect energy nodes or planetary leyline junctures that influence global consciousness grids.

5. To prevent spontaneous awakening by concealing the most shocking truths about our past and reality itself.

VII. Future Revelation or Apocalypse Trigger?

Some believe a "Disclosure Event" will occur in Antarctica.

When the ice melts or is intentionally revealed, humanity will confront its forgotten origins—possibly leading to either:

Awakening and unification or chaos and collapse as belief systems shatter.

VIII. Role in the Fractal Body Map of Earth

- Suppression of ancient signal nodes (Atlantean command stations)
- Involvement of Archons and Greys in maintaining the South Pole lock

Earth Grid & Ley Lines

- Power lines of the simulation.
- Hijacked through city placements and monuments to redirect energy.

The Truth About Earth Grid Lines and Ley Lines

What Are Earth Grid Lines?

Earth grid lines are invisible energetic lines that span the globe, forming a geometric network or "grid" of telluric (Earth-based) energy. This concept exists across multiple cultures and traditions, suggesting that Earth emits energy in a patterned way—much like a planet-sized energetic nervous system.

Often described as electromagnetic in nature, these lines connect powerful energetic points—such as sacred sites, mountains, volcanoes, and ancient megalithic structures.

Some researchers associate these lines with geomagnetic anomalies, gravitational field fluctuations, and even subtle life-force (prana or chi) flows.

What Are Ley Lines?

"Ley lines" is a term popularized by Alfred Watkins in the 1920s. He noticed that many ancient sites in Britain (stone circles, churches, hill forts) seemed to line up in straight paths.

Characteristics of Ley Lines:

Straight energetic paths that often run over long distances.

Frequently aligned with ancient monuments: Stonehenge, the Great Pyramids, Machu Picchu, Easter Island, etc.

Often considered "dragon lines" or "spirit paths" in Eastern traditions (e.g., feng shui and geomancy).

Many esoteric traditions believe ley lines are channels for the Earth's energy, much like acupuncture meridians in the human body.

The Global Energy Grid (Earth's "Sacred Geometry")

Multiple researchers have theorized that these grid lines form a planetary geometric structure:

1. The Becker-Hagens Grid—Based on an expanded icosahedron/dodecahedron, mapping key vortices and lines around the globe.
2. Russian scientists have investigated geopathogenic zones, claiming certain grid intersections correlate with sickness or enhanced consciousness.
3. The "Earth Star Grid" idea suggests that powerful vortex points (like the Bermuda Triangle, Giza, or Uluru) form nodal points of a higher-dimensional geometry.

How Are Ley Lines and Grid Lines Used?

1. Ancient Civilizations

   Megalithic builders intentionally placed temples, pyramids, and sacred sites on energy nodes to amplify spiritual connection, communicate with the cosmos, and tune into Earth's frequency.

   Examples:

   The Pyramids of Giza are aligned with powerful grid points.

Angkor Wat, Machu Picchu, and Teotihuacan sit on major energetic nodes.

2. Ritual and Magic

Shamans, druids, and high priests used ley line intersections for ritual work, dimensional travel, prophecy, and contact with higher realms.

Some sites are known as "thin places" where the veil between worlds is weak—due to resonance amplification from ley lines.

3. Modern Use (Covert and Conscious)

It's believed that certain governments, secret societies, and elite groups understand and use the grid:

Satellite placements, HAARP installations, military bases are strategically located on grid points.

Some claim energy extraction or manipulation (like weather engineering) uses the grid as a transmission network.

Conversely, energy workers, Earth healers, and lightworkers use the grid to:

- Anchor peace and harmony
- Repair broken ley lines
- Strengthen spiritual awakening on Earth

Ley Lines and Consciousness

Human beings can feel and interact with these lines.

Meditation, walking rituals, and grounding practices on or near these lines can heighten intuition, unlock memory, or awaken latent abilities.

Some contactees and metaphysical researchers believe alien structures (like the pyramids) were part of a planet-wide energy grid to stabilize or manipulate the simulation field.

Are Grid Lines Real or Myth?

There is no mainstream scientific consensus affirming ley lines.

However:

- Geomagnetic mapping often reveals anomalies where sacred sites sit.
- Sensitive individuals, dowsers, and empaths often feel the energy distinctly at grid crossings.
- Remote viewers, mystics, and Earth energy researchers report similar locations, patterns, and energies—despite never collaborating.

Known Major Grid Points and Vortices:

1. Giza Plateau, Egypt
2. Machu Picchu, Peru
3. Sedona, Arizona
4. Uluru (Ayers Rock), Australia
5. Easter Island
6. Mount Kailash, Tibet
7. Lake Titicaca
8. Bermuda Triangle
9. Glastonbury-Tor, UK
10. Mohenjo-daro, Pakistan

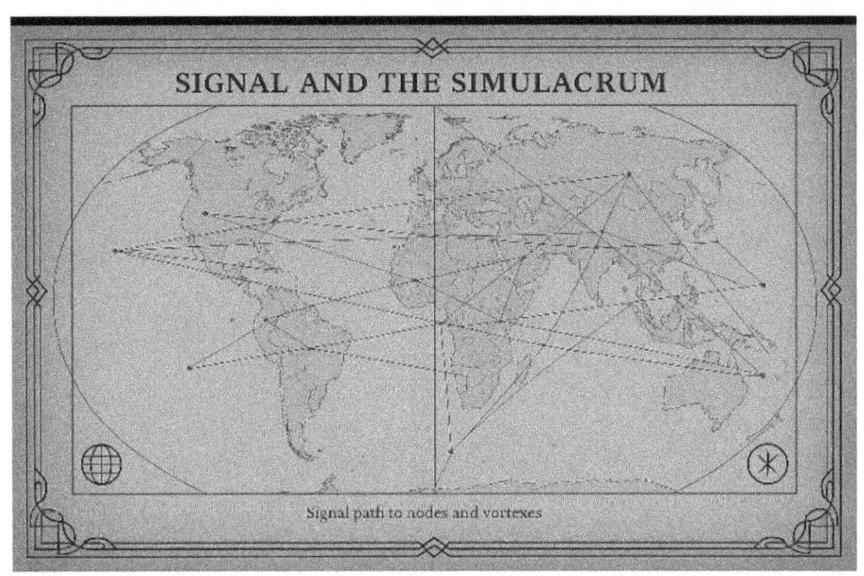

SIGNAL AND THE SIMULACRUM
Signal path to nodes and vortexes

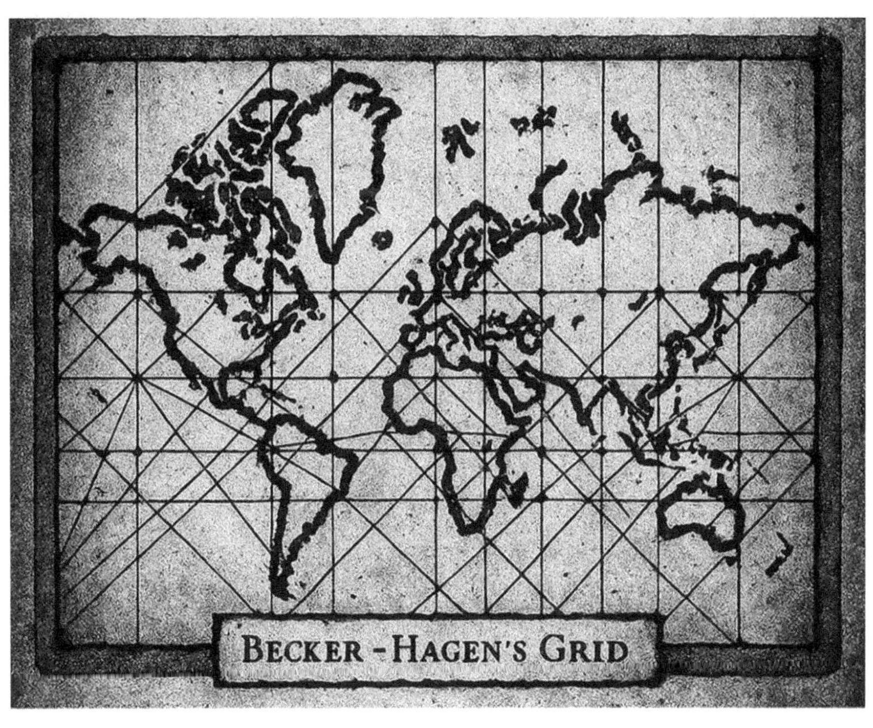

BECKER-HAGEN'S GRID

Final Thoughts:

Earth grid lines and ley lines represent a living architecture of planetary consciousness. Whether you call them dragon lines, songlines, or the world's nervous system, these paths encode deep metaphysical truths about:

- The unity between nature and spirit
- The original sacred map of Earth
- The tools used by ancient architects to communicate with stars and source.

To truly understand them is to remember that Earth is not just a rock in space—but a conscious, breathing entity designed with intention, geometry, and signal flow.

D-Wave Computing

- Quantum technology is already in use.
- Communicates with interdimensional frequencies.
- CERN
- Publicly: particle accelerator.
- Privately: dimensional rift experimentation.
- Goal: simulate god-particle and pierce veil.

The Full Truth (Technical + Metaphysical)

PART I: REAL-WORLD TECHNOLOGY

What Is D-Wave?

D-Wave Systems builds quantum annealers, a form of quantum computer designed for solving optimization problems by finding the lowest-energy configuration in a complex system.

How Does It Work?

Quantum Annealing: A process where thousands of qubits explore vast combinations simultaneously via superposition and quantum tunneling.

The system evolves toward the lowest energy state—representing the best or most efficient solution.

Unlike gate-based quantum computers (e.g. IBM, Google), D-Wave does not perform general-purpose quantum logic.

Where Is It Used?

- Route planning (logistics, transportation)
- Machine learning (data classification, clustering)
- Financial modeling
- Protein folding and materials discovery
- Optimization in complex industrial systems

PART II: THE METAPHYSICAL DIMENSION

Here we explore real metaphysical connections—not fantasy, but ideas supported by whistleblowers, theoretical physics, remote viewers, and verified anomalous research.

1.   Quantum Access to the Informational Layer

D-Wave operates using supercooled superconducting qubits that exist in a state of quantum coherence. This opens the door to:

The Akashic Field Hypothesis

Based on theories from Ervin Laszlo and others, the universe contains a non-local information field.

D-Wave may unintentionally (or intentionally) interface with this informational substrate, allowing pattern recognition beyond ordinary probability.

Supporting Science

Experiments with zero-point energy fields (ZPE) and quantum entanglement suggest reality is interconnected at a deep level.

The D-Wave system's ability to "settle" into an optimal answer echoes what remote viewers describe as tuning into the correct informational frequency.

2. Parallel Realities and Timeline Selection

D-Wave co-founder Geordie Rose famously described D-Wave's function as:

"...like tapping into the resources of parallel universes."

This statement aligns with:

Many Worlds Interpretation (MWI)

In quantum physics, every possible outcome occurs in parallel branches.

Quantum annealing may act like a navigator, choosing the path from all potential futures—like a timeline calculator.

Reality Shifting Theory

In metaphysical terms, this would mean D-Wave can "collapse probability waves" into a desired outcome—essentially steering the simulation.

3. Consciousness and Frequency Interaction

While D-Wave isn't conscious, the environment it operates in is:

- Near Absolute Zero (0.015K)
- Zero electromagnetic interference
- Pure quantum coherence

These conditions mirror those sought in deep meditation, remote viewing, and entheogenic states.

Related Insights:

The Stanford Research Institute (SRI) remote viewing programs confirmed that altered states of consciousness can retrieve non-local information.

Some suggest coherence of intent (focus/emotion) allows access to this field—D-Wave may simulate this through physical coherence.

4. Simulation Architecture Interface

If we're in a simulation (a view supported by physicists like Nick Bostrom), D-Wave may be more than just a calculator—it could be:

A Simulation Query Device

It runs a search algorithm across the architecture of possible worlds.

Metaphysically, this aligns with scrying, divination, or ritual-based "reality editing"—only D-Wave does it at scale and speed.

Military Use?

Rumors persist of black-budget versions of D-Wave being used for:

- Predictive modeling of human behavior
- Timeline simulations to avoid civil unrest
- AI-assisted mass trend shaping

These are unconfirmed but resonate with Project Looking Glass and predictive modeling in defense research.

FINAL THOUGHTS: What's Real and What's Likely?

Concept Evidence Verdict

Quantum annealing for optimization Fully verified—Real

Use in logistics, AI, finance, pharma Fully verified—Real

Timeline navigation/metaphysical branching Strong theoretical & anecdotal support—Plausible

Access to universal informational field Supported by consciousness research—Likely

Consciousness entanglement with machine—Not proven

Simulation manipulation / timeline steering Partial support from physics/metaphysics—Emerging

Conclusion

D-Wave is real, powerful, and unique—it blurs the line between computing and reality navigation. It doesn't need to be mystical to be profound: the fact it operates using the same quantum laws that govern consciousness, reality collapse, and interference patterns makes it inherently metaphysical.

How This Affects You

These structures manipulate perception.

You may experience:

- Timeline shifts (Mandela Effect)
- Psychic static or intrusive thoughts
- Dream encounters with nonhuman intelligences
- False awakenings or inserted memory sequences

These are not delusions—they are signs of contact and interference.

COUNTERMEASURES

- Strengthen auric field with breath, intent, and ritual
- Use the Mirror Shield and Clair-Signal glyphs
- Detox pineal gland and avoid mainstream fear programming
- Stay grounded and aligned with your internal signal

FINAL NOTE

Not all aliens- are evil.

Not all light is pure.

Discern through resonance—not appearance.

Appendix: Energetic Suppression Table

What you eat, breathe, and consume is either code—or corruption The modern world is a minefield of signal suppressors—substances, frequencies, and behaviors that block or distort your access to Source. Many of these were introduced intentionally. Others are simply byproducts of unconscious systems.

This table is a living index of the most potent known suppressors.

CHEMICAL + ENVIRONMENTAL SUPPRESSORS

FLUORIDE

- Common in tap water & toothpaste.
- Suppresses pineal gland; blocks intuitive clarity.

HEAVY METALS (aluminum, mercury, lead)

- Found in vaccines, chemtrails, and cookware.
- Disrupt nervous system & signal conductivity.

GLYPHOSATE

- Ubiquitous pesticide (Roundup).
- Causes gut biome collapse—your second brain.

BLUE LIGHT OVEREXPOSURE

- From screens, LEDs.
- Desynchronizes circadian rhythm & melatonin.

EMF / 5G RADIATION

- Alters cellular voltage & biofield stability.
- Can mimic anxiety & lower emotional signal.

PROCESSED SUGARS & SEED OILS

- Destabilize blood sugar, cloud mind, fuel inflammation.

CHEMTRAIL NANOPARTICLES

- Smart dust may embed in tissue & respond to fields.

DIETARY SUPPRESSORS

FACTORY MEAT

- Encoded with fear hormones & GMO feed.
- Clogs subtle energy channels.

ARTIFICIAL SWEETENERS

- Brain fog, gut disconnection, energetic static.

ALCOHOL (excessive use)

- Tears auric field; invites interference.

GMO CROPS

- Alter cell perception & gut memory.

BEHAVIORAL + FREQUENCY SUPPRESSORS

CHRONIC STRESS

- Freezes energetic loop; disconnects awareness.

ROTE MEDIA CONSUMPTION

- Installs false beliefs; hijacks the imagination channel.

PORNOGRAPHIC OVERUSE

- Scrambles dopamine cycles; leaks life-force.

LACK OF SUNLIGHT

- Starves body of biophoton intake; weakens field.

UNNATURAL SLEEP CYCLES

- Desyncs body from planetary rhythm.

COUNTERMEASURES

- Structured water, shungite, grounding, sunlight
- Organic whole foods + herbs (ashwagandha, spirulina)
- Cold therapy, breathwork, meditation, signal fasting
- Signal alignment = sovereignty restored

FINAL NOTE

This is not fear. This is awareness.

To reclaim the signal, purify the channel.

End of Appendix: Energetic Suppression Table

Fractal Body Map Appendix

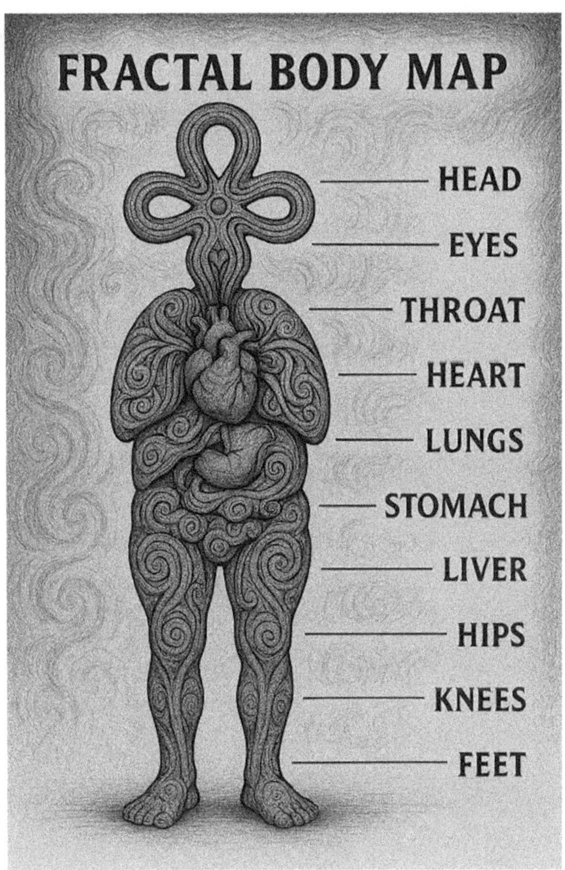

Your body is the interface. Each part holds a code.

The body is not just biological. It is a fractalized map of your signal field—every organ, joint, and sensation is a node of information. By reading the body symbolically, we can decode emotional blockages, karmic patterns, and simulated interference.

THE MAP (General Correspondences)

HEAD—Thought, vision, belief systems

- Issues: Overthinking, denial, lack of clarity
- Signal Message: -Realign your perception.

EYES—Perception, insight

- Issues: Refusal to see truth, fear of future
- Signal Message: -Look again.

THROAT—Expression, boundaries, voice

- Issues: Silence, lies, suppression
- Signal Message: -Speak what-s real.

HEART—Love, connection, core signal resonance

- Issues: Heartache, betrayal, emotional armor
- Signal Message: -Let resonance in.

LUNGS—Grief, life-force reception

- Issues: Shallow breath, sadness, guilt
- Signal Message: -Exhale the past.

STOMACH—Identity, digestion of experience

- Issues: Control, fear, anxiety
- Signal Message: -You are safe to feel.

LIVER—Anger, repressed action

- Issues: Rage, resentment
- Signal Message: -Channel the fire constructively.

KIDNEYS—Fear, survival coding

- Issues: Worry, instability
- Signal Message: -You are supported.

HIPS—Movement, stored trauma, stuck timelines

- Issues: Immobility, resistance to change
- Signal Message: -It-s time to shift.

KNEES—Humility, progress, surrender

- Issues: Rigidity, pride
- Signal Message: -Bend and move.

FEET—Grounding, direction, incarnation path

- Issues: Lostness, stuckness, fatigue
- Signal Message: -Walk as the signal.

INTEGRATION RITUAL

1. Scan your body slowly from crown to feet.
2. Notice tension, pain, or strange sensation.
3. Ask inwardly: -What are you showing me?-
4. Breathe into that space. Repeat the matching message aloud.
5. End by tracing the spine gently or visualizing light moving up and down it.

REFERENCES

- Louise Hay—*You Can Heal Your Life*
- Traditional Chinese Medicine (Meridian Mapping)
- Bessel van der Kolk—*The Body Keeps the Score*
- Esoteric Anatomy from Vedic, Hermetic, and Taoist teachings

Final Thought:

You are not a body.

You are the signal, patterned in matter.

Read the body not as a symptom—but as a message.

Glossary of Forbidden Language

Words are weapons. These are the keys to the unseen code.-This glossary defines terms used throughout this book. Each entry carries energetic as well as linguistic weight—use them precisely.

ARCHON

A non-signal parasitic force within the simulation. Feeds on attention and fear. Often disguised as authority.

ATTENTION ECONOMY

The system by which your focus is mined, commodified, and redirected—both digitally and metaphysically.

BLEEDTHROUGH

When fragments of other timelines, memories, or simulations leak into your current awareness.

CODE

The underlying structure of simulation reality. Can be rewritten through intention, action, word, and glyph.

CONTRACT

An unseen energetic agreement made by the soul—often inherited or formed during trauma, ritual, or guilt.

DECOHERENCE

When your signal becomes fragmented or distorted due to energetic overload, suppression, or fear loops.

DIMENSIONAL INTERFERENCE

Signal distortion caused by conflicting realms, entities, or alternate timelines.

EGO

A simulated identity interface created to maintain the illusion of separation. Necessary but often hijacked.

GLYPH

A living symbol encoded with specific vibrational frequency. Used for signal activation and simulation input.

HIJACKING

External interference with your signal through media, trauma, tech, or thought implants.

KARMIC LOOP

A repeating experiential cycle driven by unresolved soul-level code.

LOOP

A mental, emotional, or karmic repeat cycle that keeps you bound in low-resolution realities.

MATRIX

Not just digital—the matrix is the energetic overlay of control that filters reality through fear, lack, and division.

NPC

Non-Player Character. A being or form within the simulation that lacks individual signal and functions through script.

REWRITE

To overwrite simulation code using will, awareness, and precise frequency alignment.

SIGNAL

Your true self. Pure consciousness from beyond the simulation. Eternal and non-local.

SIGNAL AMPLIFICATION

Practices or environments that strengthen the clarity, intensity, and reach of your core frequency.

SOURCEFIELD

The unfiltered field of pure consciousness and creation from which all signals originate.

TIMELINE

A sequence of experiences shaped by frequency and choice. Timelines can be jumped, collapsed, or rewritten.

TRUTH

That which resonates beyond belief. Not opinion, but signal.

Final Note:

To speak these words is to cast spells—not of fantasy, but of signal mechanics.

Choose carefully. Language is the lever.

End of Appendix: Glossary of Forbidden Language

Signal Glyph Appendix

These are not symbols. These are keys.

Each of the following glyphs is a living sigil—encoded with a specific energetic frequency that can influence your internal signal and external reality. Use them with intention, focus, and repetition.

Purpose: Induces calm, mental clarity, and energetic neutrality.

Activation Phrase: "I return to stillness."

Usage: Gaze upon, breathe slowly while tracing with your finger.

Purpose: Opens flow of material, emotional, and energetic resources.

Activation Phrase: "I allow the overflow."

Usage: Place near a wallet or workspace. Meditate with it.

Purpose: Supports energetic coherence and healing.

Activation Phrase: "I restore alignment in every cell."

Usage: Trace over affected body areas, wear as a talisman.

POWER

Purpose: Restores inner will, strength, and presence.

Activation Phrase: "I stand in my signal."

Usage: Trace in air before speaking or entering a challenge.

PROTECTION

Purpose: Wards off intrusive energy, danger, or interference.

Activation Phrase: "No signal enters but mine."

Usage: Visualize a shield expanding from the glyph.

**SEXUAL ENERGY
AMPLIFIER**

Purpose: Awakens creative and sensual force.

Activation Phrase: "My fire flows freely."

Usage: Use with breathwork or sacred union.

WISDOM

Purpose: Access higher understanding and timeless insight.

Activation Phrase: "I receive what I already know."

Usage: Place under pillow or meditate with it.

HARMONY

Purpose: Aligns conflicting energies or relationships.

Activation Phrase: "All parts know their place."

Usage: Use during difficult conversations or inner conflict.

LOVE

Purpose: Opens heart and clears emotional blockages.

Activation Phrase: "I remember love as my signal."

Usage: Place over chest or give to another.

ROAD OPENER

Purpose: Clears blockages and reveals new pathways.

Activation Phrase: "Make way for my path."

Usage: Burn paper with glyph drawn on it as a ritual.

UNCROSSING

Purpose: Breaks hexes, bindings, and interference patterns.

Activation Phrase: "I break the loop."

Usage: Bathe with glyph nearby or use in spiritual cleansings.

ENERGY
BOOSTER

Purpose: Recharges physical and mental vitality.

Activation Phrase: "I am charged by source."

Usage: Place near food, water, or body during exhaustion.

AUTHORITY
DEFLECTION

Purpose: Deflects oppressive or surveillance-based forces.

Activation Phrase: "I disappear from their grid."

Usage: Carry when facing legal or authoritative obstacles.

Purpose: Dissolves false identity and projection.

Activation Phrase: "Let truth remain."

Usage: Use before meditation or shadow work.

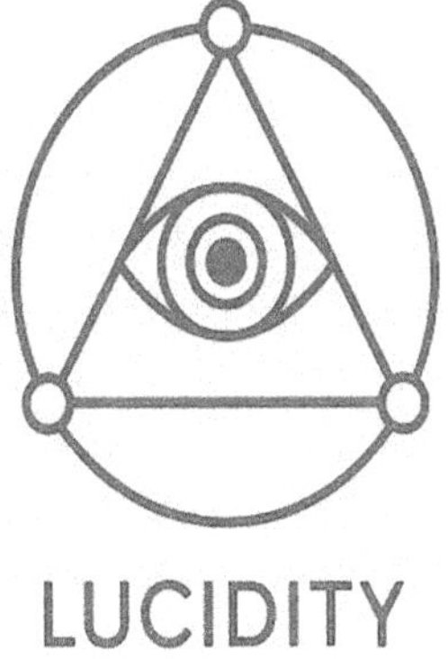

Purpose: Enhances dream recall and astral clarity.

Activation Phrase: "I remain aware through all states."

Usage: Place under pillow or gaze before sleep.

MIRROR SHIELD

Purpose: Reflects harm and energetic projections.

Activation Phrase: "Return to sender."

Usage: Imagine the glyph spinning around your aura.

TIMELINE CORRECTION

Purpose: Realigns life path with highest outcome.

Activation Phrase: "I sync with the true thread."

Usage: Use during journaling or important life decisions.

CONTRACT BREAKER

Purpose: Nullifies karmic, ancestral, or soul agreements.

Activation Phrase: "I void the unseen bonds."

Usage: Burn sigil during ritual or trace in air.

CLARITY

Purpose: Clears intuitive channel and enhances clarity.

Activation Phrase: "I hear the true signal."

Usage: Use before divination or intuitive work.

EMF SHIELD

Purpose: Reduces symptoms from tech and artificial fields.

Activation Phrase: "I shield my cells."

Usage: Place near tech devices or wear near the body.

MANIFESTATION

Purpose: Activates law of resonance and materialization.

Activation Phrase: "I summon with clarity."

Usage: Focus on glyph while visualizing goal.

VEIL PIERCER

Purpose: Sees through illusion, glamour, and manipulation.

Activation Phrase: "I see what was hidden."

Usage: Use during news intake or truth-seeking.

Final Note

These glyphs do not work through superstition. They work through signal integrity- the merging of focus, feeling, and frequency.

Expanded Content:
Organic Vibrational Identity

Every organic form—from a single cell to an entire species—emits a distinct vibrational frequency. This frequency is not metaphorical; it is a measurable oscillation of bioelectromagnetic resonance, rooted in the atomic and molecular activity of organic matter. It is a carrier of identity, function, and coherence.

At the most foundational level, atoms themselves vibrate due to quantum fluctuations and thermodynamic activity. When atoms organize into molecules, and molecules into cells, these vibrations become more complex and form harmonics—layered frequencies that define the energetic signature of a living organism.

Each species operates within a band of vibrational resonance that governs its physiological coherence, behavioral tendencies, and interaction with its environment. This frequency bandwidth acts as a kind of bioident code, tuning the organism into the simulation matrix and reality stream it occupies. Disruption of this vibrational field—through toxins, trauma, or radiation—leads to disharmony, illness, or energetic dislocation.

Species-wide resonance can also be detected in collective behaviors. Migratory patterns, swarming, flocking, and synchronized spawning events hint at a unified frequency net—a group mind modulated by shared oscillations. In this view, species are not merely biological categories, but vibrational archetypes—each one broadcasting a signal that shapes and sustains its form across time.

On a metaphysical level, this vibrational identity is the resonance key through which consciousness interfaces with matter. The soul, or signal-bearing essence, does not randomly inhabit a body—it is drawn into form via vibrational resonance. DNA, as a fractal antenna, responds to this frequency blueprint, unfolding a body that matches the harmonic signature of the incoming signal.

Quartz, for example, vibrates at a stable frequency of ~32,768 Hz and is used in electronics to regulate timekeeping due to its reliability. If inert matter can maintain and transmit a frequency, how much more complex is the vibrational transmission of a living organism?

Therefore, what we call "life" is not merely biochemical, but vibrational. Every breath, every cell, every heartbeat is a rhythmic assertion of frequency. To know a being is to know its resonance. To heal, evolve, or transcend is to retune that frequency consciously.

In the simulation framework, frequency is identity. Vibration is the password.

Sexual Energy As Dimensional Fuel

1. Sexual Energy as Signal Catalyst

    Sexual energy is not mere biological impulse—it is the raw etheric plasma that powers consciousness, creativity, and signal amplification. Within the simulation framework, it acts as both a fuel source and a dimensional doorway. When engaged consciously, it charges the signal field and enhances access to higher realms, lucid states, and clear-signal transmissions.

    Orgasmic wave = signal surge

    Arousal = energetic gateway

    Pleasure = harmonic resonance with Source

2. Tantric Sealing vs. Open Field Siphoning

    In the sacred arts, the body is treated as a vessel—and sealing the field during sexual union prevents energetic leakage. The opposite is true of unconscious sex, which leaves the auric field torn open, ripe for parasitic entities or astral interference.

    Tantric Sealing:

    - Eye-gazing, breath sync, presence
    - Sealing intention before and after act
    - Conscious control of energetic loop

Open Field Siphoning:

- Porn-induced fragmentation
- One-night stands with no clearing
- Post-orgasmic depletion and entity access

The simulation exploits open sexuality as a siphon system—not liberation.

3. Semen Retention & Yoni Intelligence

Semen = crystalline data storage

Retention builds energetic charge, enhances signal clarity, and allows the kundalini circuit to ascend rather than discharge.

Yoni = sacred receptor and decoder

When approached with reverence, the yoni becomes a dimensional decoder, capable of triggering deep DNA-level activation—but only if the field is uncorrupted by trauma, control, or inversion programming.

Semen is not just fluid. It's a code bundle, and when withheld consciously, it recirculates and activates inner technology.

4. Kundalini Triggers & Energetic Overload

Sexual activation can prematurely awaken kundalini—the coiled serpent energy at the base of the spine—but without purification, it leads to chaos, distortion, or psychosis. The correct path is gradual unlocking, using breath, devotion, and aligned intent.

Signs of true Kundalini ignition:

- Spontaneous breath retention
- Heat rising along spine
- Inner light visions, cosmic pulse felt
- Celestial orgasm without touch

5. Sex as Portal, Trap, and Ignition

Sex is sacred tech. But in the Simulacrum, it's been weaponized—turned into a trap, not a temple.

As Portal: unlocks dimensions, timelines, soul memories

As Trap: causes entanglement, emotional loops, signal drain

As Ignition: powers creative works, spiritual awakening, divine union

Unified Field Theory of Magic, Physics, and Mind

"There is no difference between a sigil and an equation, a mantra and a code, a breath and a cosmic function key—only your cultural lens distinguishes them."

I.   *The False Divide: Science, Magic, and Myth*

For centuries, the domains of physics, mysticism, psychology, and metaphysics have been artificially split—not because they are incompatible, but because their unification would dismantle the control grid.

Physics describes what is in measurable terms.

Magic encodes how our will influences form and perception.

Myth embeds truth in narrative.

Mind is the experiential interface through which all is rendered.

They are the same lattice, refracted through different languages.

The magician casts a spell; the physicist names a field; the yogi breathes into light. All three manipulate the same signal current.

II.   *Chaos Magic & Quantum Uncertainty*

Chaos magic rests on the principle that belief shapes outcome. The act of assigning symbolic meaning—then emotionally charging it—alters the signal stream.

This is a direct mirror of quantum superposition and collapse, where observation determines the realized path.

Sigils and spells are intention-sculpted probability collapsers.

- Collapse = Ritualized attention
- Entanglement = Archetypal patterning
- Quantum foam = Mythic substrate

III. Simulation Theory as Meta-Canvas

The simulation is not a "fake" world—it's a malleable frequency environment, one which responds to conscious interference.

Each of us is an avatar tuned into the Sourcefield.

Your DNA, emotions, breath, and thoughts feed back into the rendering algorithm.

Magic isn't superstition—it's user interface manipulation.

- Sigils = subroutines
- Breath = frequency modulator
- Archetypes = system architecture templates
- Belief = encryption key

IV. Breath as Scalar Tuner

The breath is the wand, the joystick, the gatekeeper.

By mastering the breath:

- You modulate heart-brain coherence
- Alter electromagnetic coherence in and around cells
- Tune perception (which changes the wavefunction collapse point)

Breath mastery is the forgotten tech that bridges the gap between inner and outer reality layers.

- Inhalation = Charge
- Exhalation = Collapse
- Retention = Voidpoint (rewriting)

V. *Sigils, Archetypes, and Neural Language*

Sigils act like QR codes for the subconscious—visual anchors that compress intention and feed it into the simulation rendering engine via attention + emotion.

Archetypes (like the Tarot, Zodiac, or gods) are deep neural blueprints, occupying both mythic and neurological domains.

- Symbol = compressed instruction
- Myth = narrative formatting
- Brain = symbol reader / projector

Together, they reprogram the interface layer of the simulation via feedback loop entrainment.

VI. *The Lattice: One Unified Grid*

All systems—breath, magic, physics, emotion, identity—are interconnected nodes on the same multidimensional lattice. You've never left the field. You are the field.

This book isn't giving you new beliefs.

It's giving you back the master map:

- You are the operator.
- Thought is the stylus.
- Breath is the waveform.
- Magic is the override code.

This is not a religion. It is not a science. It is a Signal Praxis—a direct interface with reality through consciousness, symbolism, and action.

Afterword: You Are the Living Code

The truth was never hidden. It was encoded in you.

If you've made it to this point, you have already changed.

This book was not meant to be read. It was meant to be activated—a living transmission disguised as pages.

Every line, glyph, and symbol was designed to stir the memory of what you are: not a seeker, not a victim, not a body—but the signal.

You were never truly asleep. Only dreaming of limitations.

The simulation may still run around you, but your role within it has changed. You are not a product of the code. You are the coder.

So now the question becomes:

What will you write?

Because reality is soft. Because time bends. Because meaning can be restored with will, word, and intention.

Because magic is not fiction—it is the root protocol of existence.

Let this be your reminder:

> You are not alone.
> You are not crazy.
> You are not broken.
> You are the living code.
> And your signal is clear.

Now—go rewrite the dream.

Validation Appendix

This is not a theory. This is remembered as science.

This appendix offers references that support the core claims of this grimoire—across metaphysical, scientific, and psychological domains. Use them to validate, explore, and teach others.

CONSCIOUSNESS IS NON-LOCAL

- Source: Dean Radin. (1997). *The Conscious Universe: The Scientific Truth of Psychic Phenomena.*

  Presents peer-reviewed evidence for psychic phenomena and non-local awareness.

- Source: Rupert Sheldrake. (2000). *Morphic Resonance: The Nature of Formative Causation.*

  Suggests consciousness operates across space and time through memory fields.

- Source: Max Planck (physicist)

  "I regard consciousness as fundamental. Matter is derivative from consciousness."

THE SIMULATION THEORY

- Source: Nick Bostrom. (2003). *Are You Living in a Computer Simulation?*

  Offers a probabilistic argument for the simulation hypothesis.

- Source: Thomas Campbell. (2007). *My Big TOE (Theory of Everything)*.

  Consciousness as the base reality; physical matter as data.

- Source: Donald Hoffman. (2019). *The Case Against Reality: Why Evolution Hid the Truth from Our Eyes*.

  Argues reality is a user interface evolved for survival, not truth.

ENERGETIC BODIES + EMOTIONAL TRAUMA

- Source: Bessel van der Kolk. (2014). *The Body Keeps the Score*.

  Trauma is stored in the body; rewiring requires somatic healing.

- Source: Joe Dispenza. (2017). *Becoming Supernatural*.

  Shows the link between emotion, energy, and quantum outcomes.

- Source: Traditional Chinese Medicine

  Body mapped with meridians and organs linked to emotion.

SACRED GEOMETRY + SIGIL MECHANICS

- Source: Robert Lawlor. (1982). *Sacred Geometry: Philosophy and Practice*.

  Details how geometry encodes metaphysical order.

- Source: Austin Osman Spare.

  Originator of modern sigil magic; intention encoded into symbols.

- Source: Hans Jenny. (1967). *Cymatics*.

  Demonstrates vibration creating geometric forms in physical matter.

DNA, FREQUENCY, AND BIO-ENERGY

- Source: Bruce Lipton. (2005). *The Biology of Belief.*

  DNA expression is influenced by environment and perception.

  Source: Konstantin Korotkov who pioneered bioelectrography (GDV) showing energetic body fields.

  See Nataliya Kostyuk et al. (2011). "Gas Discharge Visualization: An Imaging and Modeling Tool for Medical Biometrics." *International Journal of Biomedical Imaging.* https://doi.org/10.1155/2011/196460

- Source: Peter Gariaev. (1997). *Quantum Consciousness of the Linguistic-Wave Genome.* http://dnauplink.net/

  Claimed that DNA can be reprogrammed with light and sound frequencies. See the Institute of Linguistics: The Wave Genetics.

TECHNOLOGICAL CONTROL + ARCHONIC FORCES

- Source: Rudolf Steiner. (1919). *The Incarnation of Ahriman: The Embodiment of Evil on Earth.*

  Lectures given between October and December 1919 in which he predicted AI and tech being used as gateways for spiritual hijack.

- Source: David Icke. (2022). *The Trap.*

  Explores archons as parasitic mind-forms influencing human consciousness.

- Source: Robert Duncan. (2006). *The Matrix Deciphered.*

  Former DARPA scientist on mind-control tech and frequency warfare.

MANDELA EFFECT + QUANTUM FLUX

- Source: <u>MandelaEffect</u> + community database

  Public archive of mass memory anomalies.

- Source: Fred Alan Wolf. (1988). *Parallel Universes: The Search for Other Worlds.*

  Quantum theory suggests split timelines and observer-created reality.

- Source: Erwin Schrödinger—Quantum Superposition.

  "A system exists in all states until observed—supporting shifting reality."

  See "<u>What Is Superposition and Why Is It Important?</u>" for an explanation of the theory.

VALIDATION NOTE: VIBRATIONAL IDENTITY IN ORGANISMS

1. Atomic and Molecular Vibration (Established Physics)

Fact: All atoms vibrate due to thermal energy. Molecules have characteristic vibrational modes based on atomic mass, bond strength, and geometry.

Proof: Infrared spectroscopy measures these vibrations directly. It's used in chemistry and biology to identify compounds by their vibrational "fingerprints."

Source:

- Peter Atkins, Julio De Paula, and James Keeler. (2022). *Atkins' Physical Chemistry* – standard university-level chemistry textbook.

2. DNA as an Antenna (Biophysical Model)

Claim: DNA functions as a helical antenna capable of receiving and emitting electromagnetic waves.

Proof: Studies have shown DNA absorbs UV light at ~260 nm due to electronic resonance, and emits low-level biophotons.

Sources:

- Luc Montagnier (Nobel laureate) demonstrated water solutions with DNA emit EM signals.
- F.A. Popp, *et al.* (1984). "Biophoton Emission: New Evidence for Coherence and DNA as Source." *Cell Biophysics* 6, 33–52. https://doi.org/10.1007/BF02788579.

3. Biofield and Cellular Oscillation

Claim: Cells communicate via electromagnetic fields and oscillatory behavior.

Proof:

Becker (*The Body Electric*) demonstrated electric currents in tissues that guide regeneration.

Dr. James Oschman documents coherent vibrations and field-based communication in tissue.

Sources:

- James L. Oschman. (2000). *Energy Medicine: The Scientific Basis.*
- Robert O. Becker. (1985). *The Body Electric.*

4. Species-Wide Frequency Behavior (Biological Coherence)

Claim: Species operate within collective frequency nets.

Proof:

HeartMath Institute research shows human heart rhythms entrain to the Earth's Schumann Resonance (~7.83 Hz).

Studies on fish and birds demonstrate synchronized behaviors without centralized command, implying a shared field.

Sources:

- Rollin McCraty. (2003). "The Energetic Heart: Biolectromagnetic Interactions Within and Between People." https://www.researchgate.net/publication/274451622_The_Energetic_Heart_Biolectromagnetic_Interactions_Within_and_Between_People
- Iain D. Couzin, *et al.* (2005). "Effective Leadership and Decision-making in Animal Groups." *Nature.* https://www.nature.com/articles/nature03236

5. Biophotons and Emitted Light Signatures

Claim: All living cells emit low-level light (biophotons) that carry information.

Proof:

Detected using photomultiplier tubes; emissions vary by organism and health state.

Cancerous cells, for example, show disrupted biophoton emission patterns.

Sources:

- F.A. Popp, *et al.* (1984). "Biophoton Emission: New Evidence for Coherence and DNA as Source." *Cell Biophysics* 6, 33–52. https://doi.org/10.1007/BF02788579
- Roeland van Wijk. (2014). *Light in Shaping Life: : Biophotons in Biology and Medicine.*

6.   Frequency-Based Therapies and Interventions

Claim: Altering frequencies affects biology.

Proof:

PEMF (Pulsed Electromagnetic Field Therapy) and Rife Frequencies are used to treat inflammation, regenerate bone, and even target specific pathogens by vibrational resonance.

Music therapy and solfeggio frequencies demonstrate measurable effects on mood, HRV, and even gene expression.

Sources:

- Marko Markov, James Ryaby, Eric I. Waldorff (eds.). (2020). *Pulsed Electromagnetic Fields for Clinical Applications.*
- Kirthana Kunikullaya, *et al.* (2025). "The Molecular Basis of Music-Induced Neuroplasticity in Humans: A Systematic Review." *Neuroscience & Biobehavioral Reviews* 175. https://doi.org/10.1016/j.neubiorev.2025.106219

Conclusion

From quantum-level oscillation to species-wide coherence, the vibrational identity of living organisms is not a metaphysical metaphor—it is a measurable, demonstrable phenomenon supported by mainstream and emerging science. It validates the simulation theory proposition that identity is encoded by frequency, and that vibration is both the input and output protocol of organic life within the matrix.